Jenkins

READING-LITERATURE

SECOND READER

ADAPTED AND GRADED

BY

HARRIETTE TAYLOR TREADWELL

PRINCIPAL, WEST PULLMAN SCHOOL, CHICAGO

AND

MARGARET FREE

PRIMARY TEACHER, FORESTVILLE SCHOOL, CHICAGO, 1898-1908

ILLUSTRATED BY
FREDERICK RICHARDSON

LIVING BOOKS PRESS EDITION

EDITED BY

SHEILA CARROLL

AND

BOBBIE DAILEY

LIVING BOOKS PRESS
MOUNT PLEASANT, MICHIGAN

READING-LITERATURE SECOND READER is an unabridged edition of the original work published in 1912 by Row, Peterson & Co. Every care has been taken to faithfully reproduce the original type and illustrations, while bringing the spelling and punctuation up to date and correcting errors. The Living Books edition has also enhanced the phonics and vocabulary lists.

LIVING BOOKS PRESS™
Publishers of classic living books
5497 Gilmore Road
Mt. Pleasant, Michigan 48858
www.livingbookscurriculum.com

© 2012 Living Books Press

ISBN-13: 978-1-938192-00-5

Design and prepress by
Carrousel Graphics, Jackson, Wyoming

Printed in the United States of America

v.05.12

Living Books Press is the publishing company of Living Books Curriculum, a complete K-8 Christian homeschooling solution based on the visionary philosophy of pioneering educator Charlotte Mason. To learn more, visit our website: www.livingbookscurriculum.com.

CONTENTS

LIVING BOOKS PRESS EDITION
PREFACE

When Margaret Free and Harriette Treadwell published their Reading-Literature Series, a phonics-based reading program which included some sight-word reading and used high-quality literature rather than "twaddle," it was a great success. Their readers and the teaching guide that accompanied it were adopted by school districts across the country.

The success of the series is credited to Free and Treadwell's use of high-quality literature. Their readers start with and continually work from good literature. Phonics is used when appropriate and grows from the child's own curiosity and interaction with words:

> *After years of careful work we present these [readers] so as to utilize the child's love for stories and make an easy road to reading. Avoiding the long struggle through forced interest, and the devious byways of artificial methods, we start the child at once into the realm of good, appropriate literature.*

If you would like some guidance in the use of these readers, please see *Reading-Literature Teacher's Guide*, by Living Books Press. We hope you enjoy the readers and are as pleased as we are to see them available to a new generation of children.

SHEILA CARROLL
MOUNT PLEASANT, MICHIGAN

PURPOSE AND PLAN

Those who have examined this book, together with
The Primer and *First Reader*, should have no difficulty in
apprehending the purpose of the series, to train children in
reading and appreciating literature through reading literature.

The Primer contains nine of the best folk tales, true to the
original, and yet written in such a simple style that children
can begin reading the real story during the first week in school.
First Reader contains thirteen similar stories, of gradually
increasing difficulty, and thirty-three of the best rhymes and
jingles suitable for young children. This constitutes a course
in literature, twenty-two stories and thirty-three child poems,
as well adapted to first-grade children as are the selections for
"college entrance requirements" to high-school students.

Second Reader introduces fables and fairy stories and
continues folk tales and simple poems.

Others have used some of the same material in readers, but
in a quite different way. Their purpose seems to have been to
"mix thoroughly." We have organized our material: a group of
fables, several groups of folk and fairy stories, a group of Mother
Goose, of Rossetti, of Stevenson, and so on; so that the child may
get a body, not a mere bit, of one kind of material before passing
to another. Thus from the first he is trained to associate related
literature and to organize what he reads.

In each of *First* and *Second Readers* one story is put into
dramatic form to encourage presentation as a play. Some of
the other stories are quite as dramatic in character, and can be
dramatized by the pupils with very little help from the teacher.
Pupils always enjoy this work, and there is no better way of
securing feeling and freedom in oral expression.

With these books, besides merely learning to read, the
child has the joy of reading the best in the language, and he is
forming his taste for all subsequent reading. This development
of taste should be recognized and encouraged. From time to time
the children should be asked to choose what they would like to
reread as a class, or individuals who read well aloud may be
asked to select something already studied to read to the others.
This kind of work gives the teacher opportunity to find out what

it is in a selection that the children like, and to commend what seems to her best.

The fact that some children voluntarily memorize a story or a poem should have hearty approval. It shows abiding interest and enjoyment, and it is likely to give, for the young child at least, the maximum of literary saturation.

The cordial thanks of the authors and publishers are tendered to Mr. James M. Barrie for permission to use the exquisite selection from "Peter Pan."

THE AUTHORS

To Little Children
Learning To Read

Group of Aesop's Fables

The Wind and the Sun

The wind and the sun had a quarrel.

The wind said, "I am the stronger."

The sun said, "I am the stronger."

The wind said, "I can break trees. I move ships, and I bring the rain."

The sun said, "I bring the summer, I ripen the fruits and grains, and I cover the earth with flowers."

1

So they quarreled till they saw a man coming.

"Here comes a man with his cloak on," the wind said. "If you can take his cloak off, you shall be called the stronger. If I take it off, I shall be called the stronger."

"You begin," said the sun, and it went behind a cloud.

The wind began to blow. The man drew his cloak closer about him. The wind blew harder and harder. The man drew his cloak closer and closer. At last the wind had to give up.

Then the sun came from behind the cloud. It shone bright and warm.   The man grew warmer and warmer. He unbuttoned his cloak. He threw it back. And then he took it off.

So the sun was called the stronger.

THE FOX AND THE CROW

Once a crow was sitting on a branch of a tree with a piece of cheese in her mouth.

A fox saw the crow with the cheese. He walked up to the foot of the tree and said, "Good morning, Madam Crow. How well you look. Your feathers are glossy and your eyes are bright. You are a beautiful bird. I know you have a sweet voice. Will you sing for me? I would love to hear you sing."

The crow lifted her head and began to "caw." When she opened her mouth, the cheese fell to the ground.

"That will do," said the fox, and he snapped up the cheese and ran away.

"How foolish I was," said the crow, "to let him flatter me."

THE CROW AND THE PITCHER

One day a crow was thirsty, and he looked for some water.

He found a pitcher with water in it. But he could not reach the water with his bill.

He tried to break the pitcher, but he could not.

Then he tried to turn it over.

But he had to give that up, too.

He saw some pebbles on the ground. He picked up one pebble and dropped it into the pitcher. The water rose in the pitcher. Then he dropped in another pebble. The water rose higher. Then he dropped another and another. The water rose higher and higher.

At last he could reach it, and he drank all the water he wanted.

Where there is a will there is a way.

THE GOOSE THAT LAID
THE GOLDEN EGG

There was a man who had a very fine goose. Every day she laid an egg of gold. The man soon became rich.

As he grew rich, he grew greedy. "The goose must be gold inside," he thought to himself. "I will open her and get all the gold at once."

So he killed the goose, but he found no gold. Then the man wrung his hands and said, "I wish had been content with the golden egg each day."

THE HARE AND THE TORTOISE

"I was never beaten in a race," said a hare. "No one else can run as fast as I."

"I will run a race with you," said a tortoise.

"That is a good joke," said the hare. "I could dance around you all the way."

"Shall we run a race?" said the tortoise.

A goal was fixed and the hare was off with a bound.

"That tortoise is so slow," said the hare, "I will lie down and take a nap."

The tortoise plodded along, but she did not stop. At last she passed the hare and reached the goal.

By and by the hare awoke. He jumped up and ran as fast as he could. But when he reached the goal he found the tortoise there before him.

THE TIMID RABBITS

Some rabbits lived in the woods with other wild animals.

"What shall we do?" said a timid little rabbit. "I am afraid of those big animals. I know they will kill us."

"Let us jump into the river," said another timid rabbit. "We might better be drowned than to be killed by those big animals."

So the timid little rabbits ran as fast as they could to the river.

Some frogs heard them. The frogs were frightened and jumped into the water.

"The frogs are afraid of us," said one rabbit.

"We are all afraid of anything bigger than we are," said another. And they all ran back to the woods.

The Boy and the Wolf

Once a shepherd boy kept a flock of sheep near a village. One day he thought he would have some fun. So he ran toward the village and cried, "Help! help! the wolf is coming!"

The men from the village came running with clubs. "Where is the wolf?" they cried.

"It was only in fun," said the boy. So the men went back to their work.

A few days after this the wolf really came. He ran into the flock of sheep and began to kill them. The boy called as loud as he could, "Help! help! the wolf is here!"

"He did not tell the truth before. We cannot believe him now. He is only in fun," said the men. So not a man came to help him and many of the sheep were killed.

THE JAY AND THE PEACOCK

The peacocks lived in a large farmyard.

One day a jay flew into the farmyard and saw the feathers. He wanted to be like a peacock, so he tied the feathers to his tail and strutted about.

The peacocks saw him and were angry.

They flew at him and pecked him. At last he was glad to get away with his life.

He went back to the jays, and they were ashamed of him. They said, "Oh jay, fine feathers do not make fine birds."

THE FOX AND THE COCK

One moonlight night a fox saw a cock in a tree, but he could not reach him. So he said, "Friend Cock, I have good news."

"What is it?" said the cock.

"The lion says that no beast shall harm a bird. We must all live together as brothers."

"That is fine news," said the cock. "I am glad to hear it." Then he looked far off, and said, "Here comes a friend, we must tell him the good news."

"Who is coming?" asked the fox.

"It is our farmyard dog," said the cock. "Oh," said the fox, "I must be going."

"Do not go, Friend Fox. Stay and tell our friend the good news."

"No," said the fox, "I fear he has not heard it, and he may kill me." And away he ran as fast as he could.

THE FOX AND THE STORK

One day a fox invited a stork to dinner. The fox thought he would have some fun. So he had soup and served it in a plate.

The fox lapped the soup with his tongue, but the stork could not wet her bill.

"I am sorry, Madame Stork, that you do not like the soup," said the fox.

The stork laughed and said, "Do not be sorry. You must come to dinner with me some time."

Soon the stork invited the fox to dinner.

She had meat in a long-necked jar. The stork could get the meat with her long bill, but the fox could not get his nose into the jar.

The stork ate the meat and said, "I am sorry, Sir Fox, that you do not like the meat."

"You can have fun, too," said the fox.

THE MAN, THE BOY, AND THE DONKEY

A man and his son were going to market. It was a fine day and they were walking beside the donkey.

They had not gone far when they met a farmer. The farmer made fun of them, and said, "Why do you not ride when you have a donkey?"

So the man put the boy on the donkey. Soon they passed three old men.

"Shame, shame, you lazy boy!" they cried.

"Why do you ride and let your old father walk?"

The boy got off the donkey and the man got on.

By and by they met two old women.

"Well, well, see that lazy man!" said one old woman. "He rides and makes his little boy walk!"

Then the man took the boy on the donkey with him.

Soon they came near the market. "You are a fine pair," the people said. "A man and a big boy on one poor little donkey! Why do you not carry the donkey?"

The man and the boy got off the donkey. They tied the donkey's legs together and hung him on a long pole. Then they started to carry him over the bridge.

The donkey did not like that. He kicked himself loose and fell into the water.

"Well," said the man, "we have tried to please everybody, and we have pleased nobody. Besides we have lost our donkey."

THE LION AND THE MOUSE

One day a lion lay asleep. A little mouse ran by him. The lion awoke and put his paw on the mouse.

The little mouse was frightened, but he said, "Please let me go. If you will I may do something for you some time."

"A little mouse do something for me!" said the lion. "That could not be," but he lifted his paw and the mouse ran away.

Some time after this the lion was caught in a trap. He roared and groaned.

The little mouse heard him and came running to him. "What can I do for you?" said the mouse.

"You are too little to help me," said the lion. "These ropes are so large I cannot break them."

But the little mouse went to work and gnawed the ropes and set the lion free.

GROUP OF
MOTHER GOOSE RHYMES

COME OUT TO PLAY

Girls and boys, come out to play;
  The moon doth shine as bright as day;
Leave your supper and leave your sleep,
  And come with your playfellows into the
    street.

Come with a whoop, come with a call,
  Come with a good will or not at all.
Up the ladder and down the wall,
  A halfpenny roll will serve us all.
You find the milk, and I'll find flour,
  And we'll have a pudding in half an hour.

I Saw a Ship a-Sailing

I saw a ship a-sailing,
A-sailing on the sea;
And, oh! it was all laden
With pretty things for me!

There were comfits in the cabin,
And apples in the hold;
The sails were made of silk,
And the masts were made of gold.

The four-and-twenty sailors,
That stood between the decks,
Were four-and-twenty white mice,
With chains about their necks.

The captain was a duck,
With a packet on his back;
And when the ship began to move,
The captain said, "Quack! quack!"

Who Killed Cock Robin?

Who killed Cock Robin?
"I," said the Sparrow,
"With my bow and arrow,
I killed Cock Robin."

Who saw him die?
"I," said the Fly,
"With my little eye, I saw him die."

Who caught his blood?
"I," said the Fish, "In my little dish,
I caught his blood."

Who'll make his shroud?
"I," said the Beetle,

"With my thread and needle,
I'll make his shroud."

Who'll dig his grave?
"I," said the Owl,
"With my spade and shovel,
I'll dig his grave."

Who'll be the parson?
"I," said the Rook,
"With my little book,
I'll be the parson."

Who'll be the clerk?
"I," said the Lark,
"If it's not in the dark,
I'll be the clerk."

Who'll carry him to the grave?
"I" said the Kite
"If it's not in the night,
I'll carry him to the grave."

Who'll carry the torch?
"I," said the Linnet,
"I'll fetch it in a minute,
I'll carry the torch."

Who'll be chief mourner?
"I," said the Dove,
"For I mourn for my love,
I'll be chief mourner."

Who'll sing a song?
"I," said the Thrush,
As she sat in a bush,
"I'll sing a song."

Who'll toll the bell?
"I," said the Bull,
"Because I can pull;
So, Cock Robin, farewell."

All the birds of the air
Fell a-sighing and sobbing,
When they heard the bell toll
For poor Cock Robin.

THERE WAS A LITTLE MAN

There was a little man and he had a little gun,
And his bullets were made of lead, lead, lead;
He went to the brook, and saw a little duck,
And shot it through the head, head, head.

He carried it home to his old wife Joan,
And bade her a fire to make, make, make,
To roast the little duck he had shot in the
    brook,
And he'd go and fetch the drake, drake, drake.

The drake was a-swimming, with
    his curly tail,
The little man made it his mark, mark, mark!
He let off his gun, but he fired too soon;
And the drake flew away with a "Quack!
    quack! quack!"

THE FIR TREE

A little fir tree grew in the forest. The sun shone on it. The soft air kissed its leaves, and the dew watered its roots.

"Be happy, Oh fir tree," said the air. "Be happy, Oh fir tree," said the sunshine.

But the little tree was not happy. It took no joy in the warm sunshine. It did not hear the birds sing. It did not see the beautiful clouds above it. It wanted to be tall like the pine trees and spread out its branches. Then it could look out on the world and bow to its friends.

One day some of the pine trees were cut down. The branches were cut off and the trunks were taken out of the forest.

"Where are they going?" asked the fir tree.

"I know," said the swallow. "I saw them on great ships at sea. They were tall, stately masts, and they sailed over the seas."

"I wish I could go to sea," said the little fir tree. "I wish I could sail over the seas."

"Be happy, Oh fir tree!" said the air. "Be happy, Oh fir tree!" said the sunshine.

When Christmas time came many fir trees were taken out of the forest.

"Where are they going?" asked the little fir tree.

"I know," said the swallow. "I saw them in the houses in town. They stood in the middle of a warm room. They were covered with cakes and apples and candles and toys."

"Will they take me sometime?" asked the fir tree. "I want to go."

"Be happy, Oh fir tree!" said the air.

"Be happy, Oh fir tree!" said the sunshine.

The next Christmas the little fir tree heard a man say, "This is the prettiest tree. Let us take it." Then it was cut down and taken out of the forest.

The little fir tree was carried into a big room, where everything was light and beautiful. Some ladies came in and hung dolls and bags of candies on its branches. They hung apples and nuts all over it. They put red, white, and blue candles on it. And at the top they hung a golden star.

"How beautiful it is!" they said.

At last it was night. The wax candles were lighted, and the little fir tree trembled with joy.

Soon the door opened and the children came in. They shouted for joy when they saw the beautiful tree. And they danced about it with their new toys.

After a while the candles burned out. Nothing was left on the tree but the golden star. The children went away and the little fir tree was left alone. Then it thought of the forest, the birds, and the flowers.

—*Hans Christian Andersen*

THE DISCONTENTED PINE TREE

A little pine tree lived in a forest. Its leaves were long green needles. The sun made them shine and the wind made music through them. But the little tree was not happy. It did not like its needles.

"I wish I had beautiful leaves," it said. "I wish I had leaves of gold. Then I would be the most beautiful tree in the forest."

The fairy of the forest heard the wish of the pine tree. The next morning the tree had leaves of bright gold.

"How beautiful I am!" it said. "How my leaves sparkle in the sun! Now I shall be happy."

But soon a man came through the woods and picked all the golden leaves and left the tree bare.

The little tree was sad and it said, "I wish I had leaves of glass. They would sparkle in the sun, and no one would take them away."

The fairy heard what the tree said and the next morning it had leaves of glass. They sparkled in the sunshine and looked like diamonds.

"Now I am the prettiest tree in the forest," it said.

Soon a wind began to blow and the rain fell. The tree shivered and shook.

When the rain was over every leaf was broken. Again the little tree stood in the bare sunlight.

"I wish I had leaves like other trees. I wish I had big green leaves," said the little tree.

So the fairy gave it big green leaves.

"Now I shall be happy," it said. "Men will not want these leaves and the wind cannot break them."

But soon a goat came along with her kids and ate every leaf.

Then the pine tree sighed and said, "I wish I had my own long green needles." And next morning the little tree had its long green needles again. The birds flew back to the tree and the wind made music in its branches.

"Needles are best for pine trees," said the little tree. And it was never unhappy again.

—*German Fairy Tale*

Boots and His Brothers

Once there was a man who had three sons. The eldest son was called Peter, the next was called Paul, and the youngest was called Boots. They lived in the woods near the king's palace.

The palace stood on a hill. The hill was so rocky that no one could dig a well for the king.

A great oak tree grew nearby. The tree was so large that it made the palace dark. No one could cut it down, for every time a chip was cut out two chips grew in its place.

The king said, "The man who can dig a well and cut down the tree shall have my daughter and half my kingdom."

Many young men came to try their luck, but the tree grew bigger and stronger, and the rock did not get any softer.

Peter, Paul, and Boots wanted to try their luck. So one day they set off for the king's

palace. Soon they came to a high hill. It was covered with fir trees.

They heard something hewing and hacking up on the hill.

"I wonder what that is, hewing and hacking up there?" said Boots.

"Oh, it is only a woodcutter," said his brothers.

"Well, I want to see what it is," said Boots, and up the hill he went. And what do you think he saw? Only an axe hewing and hacking!

"Good morning," said Boots. "So here you stand hewing and hacking, do you?"

"Yes, here I have been hewing and hacking a long time, waiting for you,"said the axe.

"Well, here I am at last," said Boots, and he put the axe into his wallet. Then he went down the hill to his brothers. "What did you see up there?" they said.

"It was only an axe," said Boots.

They went on a bit of the way and came to a steep rock. There they heard something digging and delving.

"I wonder what that is, digging and delving up there?" said Boots.

"It is only a woodpecker," said Peter and Paul.

"I want to see what it is," said Boots, so up he went to the top of the rock. And what do you think he saw? Only a spade digging and delving.

"Good morning," said Boots. "So here you stand digging and delving, do you?"

"Here I have been digging and delving a long time, waiting for you," said the spade.

"Well, here I am at last," said Boots, and he put the spade into his wallet. Then he went down the hill to his brothers.

"What did you find there?" said his brothers.

"Oh, it was only a spade," said Boots.

So they went on till they came to a brook. Here they all stooped for a drink.

"I wonder where all this water comes from?" said Boots.

"Don't you know that water comes from a spring in the ground?" said his brother.

"Well, I want to see where this brook comes from," said Boots.

So he went up the brook. It grew smaller and smaller. And what do you think he saw? Only a walnut with water trickling out of it.

"Good day," said Boots. "So here you are trickling and running, are you?"

"Yes, here I have been trickling and

running a long time, waiting for you," said the walnut.

"Well, here I am at last," said Boots. He put some moss into the hole so the water could not run out. Then he put the walnut into his wallet and ran down the hill to his brothers.

"Well, where did the water come from?" said his brothers.

"Oh, it ran from a hole," he answered, "and I had the fun of seeing it."

Then they went on to the king's palace. Many young men were there trying their luck. They all wanted the king's daughter and half the kingdom. But every time a chip was cut out two grew in its place. So the tree grew bigger and stronger and the rock grew no softer.

At last the king said, "The man who fails to cut down the tree or dig the well shall be sent out of my kingdom."

This did not frighten the three brothers. Peter tried first, but two chips grew for every one he cut out. So he was sent out of the kingdom. Then Paul tried, and he had the same luck.

Now it was Boots' turn.

"Are you not afraid?" asked the king. "No,

I want to try," said Boots. Then he took the axe out of his wallet and said, "Hew and hack." And it began to hew and hack.

The chips flew, and down came the tree.

Then Boots took his spade out of his wallet and said, "Dig and delve." And the spade began to dig and delve. Soon there was a deep well.

Then Boots took the walnut out of his wallet. He pulled the moss out of the hole and laid the walnut in the well.

"Trickle and run," said Boots. And the water began to trickle and run. Soon the well was full of water.

So Boots got the king's daughter and half the kingdom.

—*Norse Folk Tale*

THE ELVES AND THE SHOEMAKER

Once upon a time there was a shoemaker. He was a good man and worked hard. Still he was poor. One day he had only one piece of leather and no money.

He cut a pair of shoes out of the leather and laid them on the table.

"It is late," he said, "I will get up early in the morning and make the shoes."

But the next morning there stood a pair of shoes on the table. They were well made. Every stitch was in the right place.

Soon a man came in. The shoes pleased him. So he bought them and paid a big price for them.

The shoemaker bought enough leather for two pairs of shoes. That night he cut them out and laid them on the table. And the next morning there stood two pairs of shoes.

Two men came in that day. "These are fine shoes," they said; and they paid a good price for them.

This time the shoemaker bought enough leather for four pairs of shoes. Again he cut them out and laid them on the table. The next morning there stood four pairs of shoes.

And so it went on. Each night he cut out his leather. Each morning he found the shoes with every stitch in the right place. Each day he sold them and bought more leather. At last he became rich.

One night just before Christmas, he said to his wife, "Let us sit up tonight and see who does our work." So they hid behind the door.

At midnight in came two little elves, skipping and jumping. They ran to the table and sat down. They took up the leather and began to stitch and hammer. The shoemaker could not take his eyes off them. The little elves worked till the shoes were made. Then they placed them on the table and away they ran.

The next morning the Shoemaker's wife said, "These little elves have made us rich, let us do something for them. I will make coats and trousers for them and you make some shoes."

So the shoemaker made two little pairs of shoes, and his good wife made two little coats and two little pairs of trousers. That night they laid them on the table and hid behind the door again.

At midnight in came the two little elves, skipping and jumping. They jumped upon the table and sat down to work. They looked about for the leather and saw none. Then they saw the little clothes. They put them on and danced for joy.

At last they jumped from the table, ran out the door, and skipped away. No one has ever seen them since. But the shoemaker and his wife are always happy at their work.

—*German Folk Tale*

CINDERELLA

Once upon a time a man had three daughters.

The youngest was beautiful and good.

She washed the dishes and the pots. She scrubbed the floors and the stairs. And she did all the work of the house. When her work was done she sat in the chimney corner among the cinders. So they called her Cinderella.

The two older sisters were proud and haughty. They wore fine dresses. But Cinderella, in her old clothes, was more beautiful than they were.

Now, the king's son gave a ball and the two older sisters were invited. They had new gowns and ribbons and laces and jewels. They could talk of nothing but the ball and their dresses.

At last the happy day came. Cinderella helped her sisters comb their hair and dress for the ball. Then they set off for the ball in a coach.

Cinderella watched them out of sight. Then she began to cry. All at once her fairy godmother appeared.

"Why are you crying, my little girl?"

"I wish–I wish–" said Cinderella, but she could not say any more.

"Do you wish you could go to the ball?" said the godmother.

"Yes," said Cinderella.

"You are a good girl and you shall go," said her godmother. "Run into the garden and get a pumpkin."

Cinderella ran to the garden and got the finest pumpkin there. The fairy godmother scooped out the inside. Then she touched it with her wand, and the pumpkin at once became a gilded coach.

"Now bring me the mousetrap," she said.

Cinderella brought the trap from the pantry.

She lifted the door and six little mice ran out. The fairy touched them with her wand and they turned into six gray horses.

"There is no coachman," she said.

"I will get the rat trap," said Cinderella. "A rat will make a fine coachman."

"So it will," said the fairy. "Run and bring it, my dear."

Cinderella brought the trap, and there were three big rats in it. The fairy chose the one with the longest whiskers. She touched him with her wand and he turned into a fat jolly coachman.

"Now bring me six lizards. You will find them behind the watering pot in the garden," said the fairy.

Cinderella found the lizards. The fairy touched them with her wand and they turned into six footmen.

"Here is your coach and six footmen," said the fairy.

Cinderella looked down at her old clothes.

The fairy touched her dress with her wand, and it became cloth of gold and silver. Her jewels were beautiful, and her little glass slippers were the prettiest in the world.

"Now," said the fairy, "you can go to the ball. But you must remember to return before midnight. For at twelve o'clock your coach will be a pumpkin. Your horses will be mice. Your coachman will be a rat. Your footmen will be lizards. And you will be Cinderella again in your ragged dress."

Cinderella said, "I will remember," and got into the coach. Away she drove as happy as a queen.

At the ball they thought a great princess had come. The king's son came out to meet her. He gave her his hand and led her into the ballroom. The music and dancing stopped. Everyone looked at the beautiful princess.

The prince led her to the seat of honor. Then he asked her to dance. Everyone said, "How beautiful she is!"

At last the king's son led Cinderella to the banquet hall. The tables were full of good things to eat, but the prince could not eat. He could not take his eyes away from the beautiful princess.

She sat down by her sisters and talked to them. They were proud to have the princess with them. But they did not know that she was Cinderella.

Soon she heard the clock strike the quarter before twelve. She hurried home as fast as she could and thanked her godmother. Then she told her that the king's son had asked her to come to the ball the next night.

Just then her sisters came home. "We have seen the most beautiful princess in the world," they said, "and she was very kind to us."

"Who was she?" asked Cinderella.

"No one knows," they said, "but the prince would give the world to know."

The next night the two sisters went to the ball. So did Cinderella, and her dress was more beautiful than before. The king's son never left her side. He said so many lovely things to her that she forgot to go home before midnight.

All at once she heard the clock begin to strike. She sprang up and ran like a deer. The prince followed her. She dropped one of her slippers on the steps and he picked it up.

"Have you seen a princess pass this way?" he asked the guards.

"No," they answered, "but we have seen a little cinder maid."

The next day the king's son sent a

messenger throughout the city. He had the slipper, and he shouted through a trumpet, "The prince will marry the maiden who can wear this slipper."

All the ladies of the king's court tried to put it on, but it was too small. The two sisters tried, but it was too small for them.

Then Cinderella said, "Let me try."

The sisters laughed at her, but the messenger said she might try. So she sat down and he put the slipper on her foot. She took the other slipper from her pocket and put it on. They fitted like wax.

Then her fairy godmother came in. She touched Cinderella, and she was more

beautifully dressed than before.

Her sisters saw that she was the beautiful princess. They fell at her feet and begged her to forgive them.

Cinderella was as good as she was beautiful. She forgave them with all her heart. Then she married the prince and took her sisters to live at the court.

—*Grimm Brothers*

HANS IN LUCK

"Master, I have served you now seven years," said Hans. "My time is up; I want to go home to my mother. Please give me my wages."

"You have served me well," said his master, and he gave him a lump of gold as big as his head.

Hans tied the gold in his handkerchief, threw it over his shoulder, and set off for home.

Soon a man came trotting along on a horse.

"A horse is a fine thing!" said Hans. "That man can go so fast, and he saves his shoes, too."

The man heard Hans. He stopped and said, "Why do you walk, my fine fellow?"

"I cannot help myself," said Hans. "I must walk because I have no horse. This lump of gold is heavy, and it hurts my shoulders."

"Let us change. I will give you my horse for your gold," said the man.

"Thank you with all my heart," said Hans.

The man took the lump of gold, and Hans got upon the horse.

"When you want to go fast you must click your tongue and say, 'Gee up! gee up!'" said the man.

Hans rode off. After a while he wanted to ride faster, so he clicked his tongue and said, "Gee up! gee up!"

The horse began to trot, and Hans fell off into the ditch. The horse ran on. A man with a cow caught the horse and brought him back to Hans.

Hans got on his feet and said, "Riding is bad sport. You are not safe. I shall never try that again. I would like a cow like yours. You can walk behind her, and you can have milk and butter and cheese. I would like to have a cow like yours."

"Well," said the man, "I will give you my cow for your horse."

"Thank you with all my heart," said Hans.

The man jumped into the saddle and was soon out of sight.

Hans was well pleased with his bargain. He drove the cow along and thought, "Now I shall have butter and cheese with my bread. When I am thirsty I can milk my cow."

Hans went on. It was noon and the sun was hot. He began to get hungry and thirsty. "I will milk my cow and have a drink," he said.

So he tied the cow to a tree. He used his hat for a pail and began to milk. Not a drop could he squeeze out. But the cow gave Hans a kick and he fell over.

Soon a butcher came by with a pig.

"What is the matter?" cried he, and he helped Hans to his feet. Hans told him about the cow.

"Of course the cow will give no milk," said the man, "she is old and only fit for the butcher."

"Well," said Hans, "I never thought of that. I will kill her and have some meat. But I do not care for cow's meat, I would like a young pig like yours. It would taste much better. Then there is the sausage."

"Well, I will give my pig for your cow," said the butcher.

"I thank you with all my heart," said Hans. He gave the cow to the butcher and went off with the pig.

After a while he met a boy with a fine white goose. They said "Good day" to each other, and Hans began to tell him how lucky he was.

Then the boy showed him his fat goose.

"I have been stuffing it for eight weeks," he said. "Feel how heavy it is. Whoever eats this roast goose will wipe the fat off his mouth."

Hans lifted the goose and said, "It is a fat goose, but my pig is fat, too."

Then the boy shook his head and said, "The mayor of our village has lost his pig. Someone stole it from the sty. And this pig looks like his. The mayor has sent some men to hunt for it. It will be bad for you if they find you with it. They will put you in the black hole."

Poor Hans grew pale with fright. "Oh dear! Oh dear!" he cried, "help me out of this trouble. I am a stranger. Take my pig and give me your goose."

"I will be running a risk," said the boy, "but for your sake I will do it." So he took the pig and walked home.

Hans took the goose under his arm and went on. "I shall have a good roast. I shall have fat for my bread and feathers for my pillow. I am in luck after all."

As Hans came near the village he saw a

knife grinder. The man was whirling his wheel and singing,

> My scissors I grind and my wheel I turn;
> And all good fellows my trade should
>   learn.

Hans stopped and said, "You seem well off."

"Yes," said the knife grinder, "my work pays well. Every time I put my hand into my pocket I find money there. But where did you get your fine goose?"

"I gave my pig for it," said Hans.

"And where did you get the pig?

"I gave my cow for it."

"And where did you get the cow?"

"I gave my horse for it."

"And where did you get the horse?"

"I gave my lump of gold for it."

"And where did you get the gold?"

"That was my pay for seven years' work."

"You seem to be in good luck," said the knife grinder. "Now, put money in your pocket and your fortune is made."

"How can I do that?" asked Hans. "You

must be a knife grinder," said the fellow. "You must have a grindstone. Here is one. I will give it to you for your goose."

"I am the luckiest fellow in the world," said Hans. So he gave his goose for the grindstone and went on.

After a while Hans got very tired and thirsty. The stone became heavier and heavier. At last he came to a stream of clear water. He stooped to get a drink, and the grindstone fell into the water with a splash.

When Hans saw the stone fall he jumped up and shouted, "I am lucky to get rid of that heavy stone."

So he went home to his mother with a light heart.

—*Grimm Brothers*

Group of
Christina G. Rossetti's Poems

A Linnet

A linnet in a gilded cage,
　　A linnet on a bough,
In frosty winter one might doubt
　　Which bird is luckier now.

But let the trees burst out in leaf,
　　And nests be on the bough,
Which linnet is the luckier bird,
　　Oh, who could doubt it now?

WHAT IS PINK?

What is pink? A rose is pink,
By the fountain's brink.

What is red? A poppy's red,
In its barley bed.

What is blue? The sky is blue,
Where the clouds float through.

What is white? A swan is white,
Sailing in the light.

What is yellow? Pears are yellow,
Rich and ripe and mellow.

What is green? The grass is green,
With small flowers between.

What is violet? Clouds are violet,
In the summer twilight.

What is orange? Why, an orange,
Just an orange!

IN THE MEADOW

In the meadow—what is in the meadow?
Bluebells, buttercups, meadow sweet,
And fairy rings for children's feet,
    In the meadow.

DAISIES

Where the pretty bright-eyed daisies are,
    With blades of grass between,
Each daisy stands up like a star
    Out of a sky of green.

A DIAMOND OR A COAL

A diamond or a coal?
    A diamond, if you please;
Who cares about a clumsy coal
    Beneath the summer trees?

A diamond or a coal?
    A coal, sir, if you please;
One comes to care about the coal
    At times when waters freeze.

AN EMERALD IS AS GREEN AS GRASS

An emerald is as green as grass;
    A ruby, red as blood;
A sapphire shines as blue as heaven;
    A flint lies in the mud.

A diamond is a brilliant stone
    To catch the world's desire;
An opal holds a fiery spark;
    But a flint holds fire.

THE PEACH TREE

The peach tree on the southern wall
    Has basked so long beneath the sun,
Her score of peaches great and small
    Bloom rosy, every one.
A peach for brother, one for each,
    A peach for you and a peach for me;
But the biggest, rosiest, downiest peach
    For Grandmamma with her tea.

THE WIND

Who has seen the wind?
    Neither I nor you;
But when the leaves hang trembling
    The wind is passing through.

Who has seen the wind?
    Neither you nor I;
But when the trees bow down their heads
    The wind is passing by.

Boats Sail on the Rivers

Boats sail on the rivers,
    And ships sail on the seas;
But clouds that sail across the sky
    Are prettier far than these.

There are bridges on the rivers,
    As pretty as you please;
But the bow that bridges heaven,
    And overtops the trees,
And builds a road from earth to sky,
    Is prettier far than these.

THE BIRTHDAY GIFT

What can I give him,
Poor as I am?
If I were a shepherd,
I would bring a lamb.
If I were a wise man,
I would do my part.
Yet what can I give him?
　Give my heart.

THE LAMBKINS

What can lambkins do,
　All the keen night through?
Nestle by their woolly mother,
　The careful ewe.

What can nestlings do
　In the nightly dew?
Sleep beneath their mother's wing
　Till day breaks anew.

THE QUEEN BEE

Once upon a time three brothers went out to seek their fortune. On the way they came to an ant hill.

"Let us turn this hill over," said the oldest brother. "It will be fun to see the ants run. They will be frightened and will try to carry their eggs away with them."

"Leave them alone," said the youngest brother. "I do not like to see them in trouble."

The brothers went on. Soon they came to a lake. Many ducks were swimming in the water.

"Let us catch some of these ducks," said one of the brothers. "They will make a fine roast."

"Leave them alone," said the youngest brother. "I do not like to see them killed."

So the brothers went on. They came to a

bees' nest in a tree. The honey ran down the
trunk of the tree.

The oldest brother said, "Let us light a fire
under the tree and smother the bees. Then we
can have the honey."

"Leave the poor bees alone," said the
youngest brother. "I do not like to see them
killed."

Again they went on, and they came to a
castle. Everything in the castle was stone. The
brothers went all through the castle.

At last they came to a door with three
locks. The center of the door was glass. They
looked in and saw an old man sitting at a
table. They called to him once. They called to

him twice. They called to him three times.

The third time he rose up, opened the three locks, and came out. He did not speak, but he led them to a table on which there were all sorts of good things to eat. They ate and drank all they wanted. Then the man gave them a place to sleep.

The next morning the man came to the oldest brother. He did not speak but led him to a stone table. On the table he read, "In the woods, under the moss are some pearls. They belong to the King's daughter. There are a thousand of them.

"If you can find them before the sun goes down you will take away the magic spell from the castle. If you try and fail you will be turned into stone."

"I will try," said the oldest brother. He went out and worked all day. When the sun went down he had only one hundred pearls. So he was turned into stone.

The next morning the old man took the second brother to the table. He read the same words and said, "I will try." He worked all day, but when the sun went down he had only two hundred pearls. So he was turned to stone.

The third morning the old man went to the youngest brother and showed him the table. "I cannot find so many pearls in one day," said he. But the old man said, "You must try."

The lad went to the woods. "I wonder if I can find a thousand pearls in one day," he said. "Well, I must try."

Just then he saw the ant King coming toward him. He had five thousand ants with him. They came from the ant hill which he had saved.

Soon the ants found all the pearls.

They piled them in a heap and went home. They had thanked the boy for saving their lives.

The boy took the pearls to the old man.

"I have another task for you," said the old man. "You must bring me the key to the princess's room. It is at the bottom of the lake."

The boy went down to the shore of the lake. The ducks saw him and knew him. They swam to him and asked him what he wanted.

He told them about the key at the bottom of the lake. The ducks dived to the bottom of the lake and brought the key to him. The lad took it to the old man.

"There is one more task for you," said the old man. "The King's daughters are all asleep in the castle. You must find the youngest daughter and awake her. They all look alike. But before they went to sleep the oldest one ate barley sugar, the second one ate syrup, and the youngest one ate honey."

The boy went into the castle. He found the three daughters. While he was wondering which one was the youngest, the queen bee flew in. She went to the mouths of the three sleepers. Then she settled on one.

The boy knew this was the one who had eaten the honey. He awoke her and the spell was broken. Then all awoke from their sleep.

The youngest brother married the youngest daughter. His brothers married the other daughters of the King, and they all lived happily ever after.

—*German Fairy Tale*

THE BRAVE TIN SOLDIER

"Tin soldiers! Tin soldiers!" cried a little boy, clapping his hands. He set them down on the table. There were twenty-five tin soldiers, all exactly alike except one. That one had been made last, and there was not enough tin to finish him. He had only one leg, but he stood firm on that.

Just in front of this brave Tin Soldier was a paper castle with trees around it. Before it was a little lake with swans on it. The Tin Soldier looked into the window, and there he saw a little paper lady. She was dancing, and she wore a white lace dress with a blue scarf over her shoulder. She stretched out both arms and lifted one leg. The Tin Soldier thought she had but one leg like himself.

"That is the mate for me," he said, "but she lives in a grand castle and I live in a tin box.

There are twenty-five of us, too. It is no place for a beautiful lady, but I must know her."

So he lay down behind the snuffbox where he could watch the little paper lady.

"She wants to know me, too," thought he.

That night all the other tin soldiers were put into the box, and the little boy went to bed. Then all the toys on the table began to play. They played 'Visiting' and 'War,' and they had parties. The nutcracker turned somersaults, and the pencils ran races. The tin soldiers rattled in their box.

They wanted to play, too, but they could not lift the lid.

The brave Tin Soldier stood up firm on his

one leg, and never took his eyes off the little dancer. The little lady stood on one foot with her arms stretched out to the Tin Soldier.

The clock struck twelve, and bounce! Off flew the lid of the snuffbox. There stood a little black goblin.

"Tin Soldier," said the goblin, "don't stare so. She does not belong to you."

The Tin Soldier never turned his head.

"Just wait till tomorrow," said the goblin.

The next morning the little boy put the Tin Soldier in the window. "Now I cannot see the little lady," said he. "I wonder if this is what the goblin meant when he said, 'Just wait till tomorrow.'" Suddenly the window opened and out went the Tin Soldier to the ground. He put his leg straight up and struck the ground with his musket.

The boy ran to get him, but he could not see him. "If I cried, 'Here I am,' he might find me, but a soldier in uniform never cries," thought the brave Tin Soldier.

Now it began to rain. The drops fell faster and faster. At last the rain came down in torrents. When it was over two boys came by. "Look!" said one of them, "there lies a tin soldier. Let us give him a ride in a boat."

They made a boat of a newspaper and put the Tin Soldier into it. He stood up bravely, shouldered his musket, and sailed down the gutter. The two boys ran beside him and clapped their hands. The boat rocked up and down and turned round and round, but the brave Tin Soldier looked straight ahead and held his musket.

All at once the boat went into a dark channel. "Where am I going now? This is that goblin's doings," said he. "This is what he meant when he said, 'Wait till tomorrow.' I wonder what he will do next."

Just then a great rat called out, "Give me your passport"; but the Tin Soldier never turned his head. "Hold him! Hold him!" cried the rat. "He has not paid his toll." The Tin Soldier held his musket tighter.

Soon he heard a roaring noise. The boat went on. It whirled over three or four times, then down it went over a waterfall. The boat was filled with water. It sank deeper and deeper, and the water closed over the Tin Soldier's head.

"I shall never see the little lady again,"

said he. He thought he heard her say, "Farewell, brave Tin Soldier!"

Just then a great fish snapped him up. It was darker than ever, but the brave Tin Soldier lay still and held his musket. The fish swam to and fro. Suddenly he was jerked up.

The fish had been caught. It was taken into the kitchen and the cook opened it.

"The Tin Soldier!" she cried.

Then she carried him into the playroom and put him on the table. The Tin Soldier looked around. There stood the castle with the little lady. She was still standing on one foot and stretching her arms out to him. He looked at her and thought, "She is glad to see me"; but he said nothing.

Then he looked at the snuffbox and wondered what the goblin would do now.

Just then the boy picked up the Tin Soldier and threw him into the stove. "This is the goblin's work," the Tin Soldier said to himself. Then he looked at the little lady and she looked at him. He felt that he was melting, but he stood firm and shouldered his musket.

Suddenly the wind caught up the little lady and she flew into the stove with the Tin

Soldier. Then she flashed up in a flame and was gone. The Tin Soldier melted down into a lump. When they took him out with the ashes he was in the shape of a tin heart.

—*Hans Christian Andersen*

THE SISTER OF THE SUN

Lars was the son of a gardener who worked for the king. He was quiet and well-behaved, so the king let him come to the palace to play with the prince.

Once the king gave the two boys bows and arrows exactly alike. When the prince's lessons were done they would go to the playground to see who could shoot the higher.

One morning they let their arrows fly together. The arrows went so high that they were out of sight, and the boys thought they were lost. Soon, however, they fell to the ground and the tail feather of a golden hen was sticking in one of them.

"That is my arrow," said the prince.

"No, it is mine," said Lars.

The boys could not agree, so they went to the king.

"The feather must belong to the prince," said the king; "no peasant boy could bring down such a bird."

But Lars would not listen to this. He said, "I know the feather is on my arrow."

"Very well," said the king, "the feather shall be yours if you can catch the golden hen that lost the feather; but if you fail to catch her, you shall lose your head."

Lars was frightened at the king's words. He did not know where to look for the golden hen, but he must obey the king. So he went home and put some food into a bag and set off. He went to all the farmyards. There were red hens and brown hens and white hens, but there were no golden hens. At last he met a fox who was very friendly. "Where are you going?" asked the fox.

"I must find the golden hen that lost a tail feather," answered Lars, "but I don't know where she lives or how to catch her."

The fox smelled of the feathers. Then he said, "I know every farmyard in the world. That golden hen belongs to the Sister of the Sun. She lives far in the east. Come with me. I will show you the way."

So Lars and the fox walked together for days. At last they came to a great palace. "This is the place," said the fox. "I think it would be better for me to go in. I know better how to catch hens than you do."

"No," answered Lars, "I must catch the golden hen myself."

"Well, go on then," said the fox, "but be careful. Take only the hen that lost a feather." So Lars went through the palace gate. He soon saw three golden hens strutting about. As the last one passed him he saw a tail feather was gone.

Lars jumped forward and caught the hen. He tucked her under his arm and started for the gate. Just as he reached the gate he looked back into the palace.

"There is no hurry," he said, "I may as well see something more while I am here." So he turned back. He entered the palace and looked at all the beautiful things. Soon he came to a room of blue and gold, and there lay a beautiful maiden. "How lovely she is!" said he. "She must be the Sister of the Sun."

As Lars looked at the beautiful princess he forgot all about the hen and away she flew. Then Lars looked again at the sleeping princess and went away. When he tried to catch the golden hen again she would not let him come near. And worse than that, the other two hens began to cackle so loud that the Sister of the Sun awoke. She jumped up and ran to the door. "What are you doing?" she cried.

"I am trying to catch a golden hen," replied Lars.

"Oh," said the Sister of the Sun, "if you will bring back my sister, the Princess Sunset, you shall have one of my golden hens. My sister was carried away by a giant, whose castle is a long way off."

Lars left the palace and went to his friend the fox. He told him all that had happened.

"You have made a fine mess of it, but there is no time to lose," said the fox. "Let us set off at once. I know the way." Lars and the fox walked for days. At last they came to a great black castle.

"You stay outside this time," said the fox, "and I will go in and get the princess. When I bring her out you run away with her as fast as you can. Then I will return to the castle and talk to the giants and they will not miss her."

So the fox slipped into the hall. There were many giants in the hall, both young and old, and they were all dancing about the princess. As soon as the giants saw the fox they cried out, "Come and dance too, Old Fox. It is a long time since we have seen you."

So the fox stood up and danced with the best of them. After a while he stopped and said, "I know a new dance; shall I show it to you?"

"Yes, show us the new dance," cried the giants.

"If Princess Sunset will do me the honor."

said the sly old fox, "you shall soon see how it
is done."

"Dance with her if you like," cried the
giants. So the fox and the princess began to
dance. Round and round they went.

Whenever they came near a candle the
fox blew it out. It grew so dark that the giants
could not see. Then the fox and the princess
danced out of the door to Lars. "Run for your
lives," he cried. Then he ran back into the hall.

The giants made a light. After a while
someone cried, "Where is the princess?"

"She is safe," replied the fox, for he knew
that Lars was now far over the mountains with
the princess. Then he sprang through the door,

crying, "Catch the princess if you can."

Now the giants knew that the princess had escaped. They ran after the fox as fast as their legs could carry them. The fox led them a merry chase, calling, "This way! This way!" He ran all night, but he did not run the way Lars had gone.

When the red light began to spread over the east he stopped and cried, "Look, there is the Princess Sunrise."

The giants looked up, but the bright light blinded them, so they could follow the fox no more. Then the fox set off to join Lars and Princess Sunset. And they all went on together till they reached the castle of Princess Sunrise.

There was great feasting at the castle when Princess Sunset returned, and they could not do enough for Lars. Princess Sunrise gave him the golden hen and told him to come back to see her.

Lars' heart was full of joy as he set off for home with the golden hen under his arm. The king could hardly believe all that Lars told him. But he said, "You must prove yourself worthy of the Sister of the Sun," so he gave him many hard tasks to perform.

Lars did everything he was bid, and after a long time he went to live in the palace with Princess Sunrise.

—*Lapland Folk Tale*

Why the Sea is Salt

Once upon a time, long ago, there were two brothers. One was rich and one was poor.

Christmas Eve came and the poor brother had no meat nor bread in his house. He went to the rich brother and asked for something to eat.

"Do what I ask you," said the rich brother, "and I will give you a ham."

"Thank you," said the poor brother, "I will do whatever you ask."

"Here is the ham, then," said the rich man. "Now, go to the home of the people who live down below."

The poor man took the ham and set off. He walked and walked till it was dark.

At last he came to an old man with a long white beard. He was standing by a big gate, chopping wood.

"Good evening," said the man with the ham. "Good evening to you," said the old man. "Where are you going with that ham?"

"I am going to the home of the people who live down below," answered the poor man.

"Here you are, then," said the old man.

"But if you go down with that ham, they will want to buy it. Do not sell it for money, but ask for the old mill behind the door. When you come out I will teach you to use it."

So the man with the ham thanked the old man and rapped at the door.

He went in, and all the men, both great and small, came around him. They begged for the ham, and tried to outbid each other.

"This ham is for my old woman's Christmas dinner," said the poor man. "But if you will give me the old mill behind the door, I will sell it to you."

"We cannot give you the old mill," they said.

"Then I cannot give you the ham," said the poor man, and he started to go away.

Then they all cried, "Take the old mill. We must have the ham." So the man took the old mill and went out. The old man showed him how to use it, and he set off for home.

"You have been gone a long time," said his wife. "It is late, and I have had nothing to eat. Where have you been?"

"I had something to see about," said the man, "and I had a long way to go. But now see what I have."

So he set the old mill on the table and said, "Grind everything that is good for a Christmas dinner." And the mill obeyed. So it ground meat and drink and all kinds of good things.

On the third day he invited his brother and all his neighbors to dinner.

"Where did all these things come from?" said his brother. "It was only Christmas Eve that you begged me for food."

"They came from behind the door," said the man with the mill. He was so proud of the mill that he brought it from behind the door.

"There you see where my riches came from," said he. And he put it on the table, and it ground everything they asked for.

Now, the rich brother wanted the mill. "You may have it for three hundred dollars after haymaking," said the poor brother. "I can grind all the food I want before haymaking," thought he.

After haymaking the rich brother came for his mill and took it home.

The next morning he said to his wife, "You go to the field and I will get the dinner."

When dinner time came he set the mill on the table and said, "Grind herring and milk pottage, and do it quickly."

So the mill began to grind herring and milk pottage. Soon the dishes were filled. Then the tubs were filled. Then the food came out all over the kitchen floor.

The man twisted and turned the mill and cried, "Stop, stop." But the mill went on grinding. The man had forgotten to ask how to stop the mill.

Soon the kitchen was full of pottage.

He threw the door open and ran out. The fish and pottage ran out after him and ran all over the fields. The man ran as fast as he could to his brother's house!

"Take care, or you will be drowned in the pottage," he cried to his wife, as he passed by her. He ran to his brother and begged him to take the mill back.

"If it grinds another hour we shall all be drowned," he cried.

Now the poor brother had both the money and the mill. So he built a farm house larger than his brother's.

He found that the mill would grind gold. It ground so much gold that he covered his house with gold. The farm house lay close to the seashore. So it shone far out to sea.

Everyone who sailed by stopped to see the gold farmhouse, and everyone wanted to see the wonderful mill.

After a long, long time, a skipper asked if the mill would grind salt. "Yes," said the owner, "it will grind anything."

"I must have the mill," said the skipper.

The man did not want to sell it, but the skipper offered him so much money that he could not say no. So he sold the mill to the skipper.

The skipper took the mill on his back and hurried to the ship.

When he got out to sea he put the mill down and said, "Grind salt, and grind nothing but salt." So the mill began to grind salt. Soon the ship was full of salt.

The skipper tried to stop the mill, but he had forgotten to learn how to stop it. He twisted and turned it and cried, "Stop, stop," but the mill kept on grinding salt.

Before the skipper could sail to the shore, the ship became so heavy with salt that it went to the bottom of the sea. And there the mill is still grinding salt. They say that is why the sea is salt.

—*Norse Folk Tale*

THE FLYING SHIP

Once upon a time there was a rich Czar.
He had everything he could wish for.

One day he said, "If I could fly like the
birds, I should be happy."

So he called his wise men and said, "Make
me a ship that will fly like a bird." But the
wise men answered, "We do not know how to
make a flying ship."

So the Czar sent word all over the land,

"The man who brings me a flying ship shall
have my daughter and half of my kingdom."

Now, near the palace lived an old man and
an old woman who had three sons.

The eldest son said, "I will go and find a

ship that can fly, then I can have the Czar's daughter and half of the kingdom." So he set off with his mother's blessing.

Then the next son said, "I shall try, too," and off he set.

The two brothers went a long, long way, but they found no flying ship.

Then Ivan, the youngest son, said, "I must find the flying ship."

"No, my son," said his mother, "you are too young to go."

But Ivan kept saying, "I must go! I must go!" So his mother gave him her blessing and he set off.

He went a long way, and at last he met an old man. "Where are you going, my lad?" said the old man.

"I am going to get a flying ship for the Czar," replied Ivan.

"And can you make a flying ship?" asked the old man.

"No, I cannot make one, but they will make one for me somewhere," answered Ivan.

"And where is that somewhere?" asked the old man.

"I do not know," said the lad.

"Well, then," said the old man, "let us sit down and eat. What have you in your knapsack?"

"There is only dry bread in it," said Ivan. "I am ashamed to show you."

"Your mother has given it to you. Do not be ashamed of it," said the old man. "Let us see what you have."

So Ivan opened his knapsack. What did he see? There lay white rolls and many kinds of meat.

"Here is a fine feast," said the old man. And they sat down on the grass and ate.

"Now," said the old man, "go into the woods. Bow three times to the first oak tree you see, and strike it with your ax. Then fall to the earth with your face down. Wait there until you hear a whirring sound. Then look up and you will see a flying ship. Get into it and fly where you like. Be kind to all you meet and take them into the ship with you."

"Thank you," said Ivan, and he went into the woods. He did just as the old man told him to do. He bowed three times before the first oak tree and struck it with his ax. Then he fell with his face to the ground. In a little while he heard a whirring sound. He looked up and there was the flying ship.

Ivan got into the ship and away it flew. And look! He saw a man lying with his ear to the ground.

"Good day, Uncle," said Ivan, "what are you doing? "

"I can hear all around the world," said the man. "My name is Sharp Ear."

"Come and ride with me," said Ivan.

"Thank you," said the man, and he climbed into the ship. Away they flew. They flew and flew. And look! There was a man hopping on one foot. The other foot was tied to his ear.

"Good day, Uncle," said Ivan. "Why do you hop on one foot? "

"Oh," said the man, "if I untie my foot I can step halfway around the world. My name is Swift Foot."

"Come and ride with us," said Ivan.

"Thank you," said Swift Foot, and he climbed into the ship. Away they flew. They flew and flew. And look! They saw a man with a gun.

"Good day, Uncle," said Ivan, "what are you shooting at? There is not a bird in sight."

"Oh," said the man, "I can hit a bird one hundred miles away. My name is Sure Shot."

"Come and ride with us," said Ivan.

"Thank you," said the man, and he climbed into the ship. Away they flew. They flew and flew. And look! There was a man with a sack of bread on his back.

"Good day, Uncle," said Ivan. "Where are you going?"

"I am going to get some bread for my dinner," answered the man.

"But you have a big sack of bread on your back," said Ivan.

"Oh, that is only a mouthful," answered the man. "They call me Gobbler."

"Come and ride with us," said Ivan.

"Thank you," said the man, and he climbed into the ship. Away they flew. They flew and flew. And look! There was a man walking by a lake.

"Good day, Uncle, what are you looking for?" said Ivan.

"I want a drink," answered the man. "I am thirsty."

"There is a whole lake of water," said the lad, "why don't you drink of that?"

"That would not make a mouthful for me," said the man. "They call me Drinker."

"Come and ride with us," said Ivan.

"Thank you," said the man, and he climbed into the ship. And away they flew. They flew and flew. And look! There was a man with a great bundle of straw on his back.

"Good day to you," said Ivan. "Where are you going with that straw?"

"I am going to the village," answered the man.

"Have they no straw in the village?" asked Ivan.

"They have no straw like this; this is magic straw," answered the man. "When it is hot I lay this straw down and it becomes cool."

"Come and ride with us," said Ivan.

"Thank you," said the man, and he climbed into the ship. Away they flew. They flew and flew. And look! There was a man with a bundle of wood on his back.

"Good day, Uncle," said Ivan, "why do you drag that bundle of wood about?"

"This is magic wood," said the man.

"If I put it on the ground a great army will spring up."

"Come and ride with us," said Ivan.

"Thank you," said the man. And he climbed into the ship. And away they flew. They flew and flew. And look! There was the Czar's castle.

The people in the castle heard the whirring sound. They ran out to see what it was. "Look," they cried, "there is the flying ship!"

The Czar looked out of the window and saw the ship. "Some great prince has won my daughter," he said. So he sent out a servant to welcome him.

Soon the servant came back. "Oh, Czar,"

said he, "there is only a poor peasant lad in the ship."

The Czar was very angry. "My daughter cannot marry a peasant. But I must have the flying ship. I must give him some hard tasks to do." So he said to his servant, "Go tell this peasant lad that he must bring me some living and singing water from the end of the world. And he must bring it before my dinner is over."

Now Sharp Ear heard the Czar's command, and he told Ivan.

"What shall I do?" asked Ivan. "It would take me a year to go to the end of the world."

"Do not be afraid," said Swift Foot.

"I will get some living and singing water for you. Untie my foot and I will step to the end of the world for it. That will be easy for me."

Just then the servant came out and gave Ivan the Czar's order. "Tell the Czar that he shall be obeyed," said Ivan.

Swift Foot was off in a minute and found the living and singing water. "I have time enough," he said, "I will rest by this old mill." So he sat down and fell asleep.

The King's dinner was almost ended, and Swift Foot had not returned. Sharp Ear put his ear to the ground. "I can hear Swift Foot snoring by the old mill," said he.

"Then I will wake him," said Sure Shot.

And he took his gun and shot into the mill. Swift Foot awoke and was at the Czar's castle in a minute.

The Czar took the water, but he was very angry. So he said to his servant,

"Go tell the lad that he must eat twenty roasted oxen and twenty tons of bread at one meal."

Again Sharp Ear heard the Czar's order and told Ivan.

"What shall I do?" asked Ivan. "It would take me twenty years to eat twenty oxen and twenty tons of bread."

"Do not be afraid," said Gobbler.

"Twenty oxen and twenty tons of bread will only make one meal for me. I will eat it."

Just then the servant came out and gave Ivan the Czar's order.

"Tell the Czar that he shall be obeyed," said Ivan.

The twenty roasted oxen and twenty tons of bread were brought to the ship and Gobbler ate it all up.

"I am still hungry," he said. "They might have given me more."

The Czar was more angry than ever. So he ordered Ivan to drink forty barrels of water. A barrel held forty pails of water.

Again Sharp Ear heard the Czar's command and told Ivan.

"What shall I do?" asked Ivan. I could not drink one pail of water."

"Do not be afraid," said Drinker. "I can drink the forty barrels at once."

The forty barrels of water were sent to the

ship. Soon it was all gone. "I am still thirsty," said Drinker.

The Czar said, "We must trick this lad." So he ordered Ivan to get ready for the wedding. "Make the iron bathroom red hot," said the Czar to his servant.

Sharp Ear heard the order and told Ivan.

"What shall I do?" said Ivan. "No one can save me now."

"Do not be afraid," said the man with the straw. "Take me with you."

Ivan went into the bathroom and the man with the straw went with him. "I must put straw on the floor," said the man.

Now the magic straw made the bathroom cool, so Ivan lay down by the stove.

In the morning the servant opened the door. He found Ivan lying by the stove singing.

When the Czar heard this he said, "What can I do? I must get rid of this peasant. He must not marry my daughter, but I must have his flying ship. I will order him to raise a large army. He cannot do that."

Again Sharp Ear heard the Czar's command and told Ivan.

"Now I am lost," said Ivan, sadly. "You cannot help me this time."

"You have forgotten me," said the man with the bundle of wood. "I will place my magic sticks around the castle, and soon you will see a great army."

The servant came and told Ivan the Czar's command.

"The Czar shall be obeyed," said Ivan. "But I must have his daughter, or my army shall break down the castle."

The Czar laughed when he heard that Ivan would break down his castle.

That night the magic wood was placed around the castle. Each piece of wood became a soldier. There stood a great army of men. Bugles sounded, drums began to beat, and the soldiers began to march.

The Czar awoke, and he looked out of the window. The soldiers presented arms.

The Czar was filled with terror. "I can do nothing against such a great army. This peasant shall have my daughter."

So he sent his royal robes and jewels to Ivan, and invited him to the castle.

Ivan put on the royal robes and jewels. He looked so handsome that the princess fell in love with him.

There was a grand wedding and a great banquet. For once Gobbler and Drinker had all they wanted to eat and drink. The Czar gave Ivan half of the kingdom, and they were all happy ever after.

—*Russian Folk Tale*

GROUP OF
ROBERT LOUIS STEVENSON'S POEMS

FAIRY LAND

When at home alone I sit
And am very tired of it,
I have just to shut my eyes
To go sailing through the skies—

To go sailing far away
To the pleasant Land of Play,
To the fairy land afar
Where the little children are.

Where the clover tops are trees,
And the rain-pools are the seas,
And the leaves like little ships
Sail about on tiny trips.

Should a leaflet come to land,
Drifting near to where I stand,
Straight I'll board that tiny boat,
Round the rain-pool sea to float.

In the forest, to and fro,
I can wander, I can go;
See the spider and the fly,
And the ants go marching by,
Carrying parcels with their feet
Down the green and grassy street.

    O dear me
    That I could be
A sailor on the rain-pool sea,
A climber on the clover tree,
And just come back, a sleepy-head,
Late at night to go to bed.

THE SWING

How do you like to go up in a swing,
  Up in the air so blue?
Oh, I do think it the pleasantest thing
  Ever a child can do!

Up in the air and over the wall,
  Till I can see so wide,
Rivers and trees and cattle and all
  Over the countryside.

Till I look down on the garden green,
  Down on the roof so brown—
Up in the air I go flying again,
  Up in the air and down.

RAIN

The rain is raining all around,
    It falls on field and tree,
It rains on the umbrellas here,
    And on the ships at sea.

SINGING

Of speckled eggs the birdie sings
    And nests among the trees;
The sailor sings of ropes and things
    In ships upon the seas.

The children sing in far Japan,
    The children sing in Spain;
The organ with the organ man
    Is singing in the rain.

At the Seaside

When I was down beside the sea
A wooden spade they gave to me
    To dig the sandy shore.

My holes were empty like a cup.
In every hole the sea came up,
    Till it could come no more.

Farewell to the Farm

The coach is at the door at last;
The eager children mounting fast
And kissing hands, in chorus sing:
Good bye, good bye, to everything!

To house and garden, field and lawn,
To meadow-gates we swung upon,
To pump and stable, tree and swing,
Good bye, good bye, to everything!

And fare you well for evermore,
O ladder at the hayloft door,

O hayloft where the cobwebs cling,
Good bye, good bye, to everything!

Crack goes the whip, and off we go;
The trees and houses smaller grow;
Last, round the woody turn we swing:
Good bye, good bye, to everything!

TIME TO RISE

A birdie with a yellow bill
Hopped upon the window-sill,
Cocked his shining eye and said:
"Are n't you 'shamed, you sleepy-head?"

WHOLE DUTY OF CHILDREN

A child should always say what's true,
And speak when he is spoken to,
And behave mannerly at table,
At least as far as he is able.

LOOKING FORWARD

When I am grown to man's estate,
I shall be very proud and great,

———⊰⊱———

Not to meddle with my toys.

BED IN SUMMER

In winter I get up at night,
And dress by yellow candle light.
In summer, quite the other way,
I have to go to bed by day.

I have to go to bed and see
The birds still hopping on the tree,
Or hear the grown-up people's feet
Still going past me on the street.

And does it not seem hard to you,
When all the sky is clear and blue,
And I should like so much to play,
To have to go to bed by day?

Where Go the Boats?

Dark brown is the river,
    Golden is the sand.
It flows along forever
    With trees on either hand.

Green leaves a-floating,
    Castles of the foam,
Boats of mine a-boating—
    Where will all come home?

On goes the river
    And out past the mill,
Away down the valley,
    Away down the hill.

Away down the river,
    A hundred miles or more,
Other little children
    Shall bring my boats ashore.

MY SHADOW

I have a little shadow,
    That goes in and out with me,
And what can be the use of him
    Is more than I can see;
He is very, very like me,
    From the heels up to the head,
And I see him jump before me,
    When I jump into my bed.

The funniest thing about him
    Is the way he likes to grow,
Not at all like proper children,
    Which is always very slow;
For he sometimes shoots up taller,
    Like an india-rubber ball,

And he sometimes gets so little
    That there's none of him at all.

He hasn't a dim notion
    Of how children ought to play,
And can only make a fool of me
    In every sort of way;
He stays so close beside me,
    He's a coward, you can see;
I'd think shame to stick to nursie
    As that shadow sticks to me!

One morning very early,
    Before the sun was up,
I rose and found the shining dew
    On every buttercup;
But my lazy little shadow,
    Like a foolish sleepy-head,
Had staid at home behind me
    And was fast asleep in bed.

Sleeping Beauty

Long ago there lived a king and queen who wished every day for a child. At last a little girl was born to them.

The king was filled with joy. He made a great feast and invited everyone in his kingdom. The twelve fairies were invited.

Now there was an old fairy who had not been seen for fifty years. Everyone had forgotten her. So she was not invited.

At the end of the feast the fairies gave the little princess magic gifts. One gave her kindness, another gave beauty, another gave riches. They gave her everything a child could wish for.

Eleven of the fairies had given their gifts when the old fairy stepped in. She was angry because she had not been invited. So she cried out, "When the princess is fifteen years old, she

shall prick her finger with a spindle and die."
Without another word she left the hall.

One fairy had not given her gift. She could
not take away the wish of the angry fairy, but
she could change it. So she said, "The princess
shall not die. But when she pricks her finger
she shall sleep a hundred years."

The king thought he could protect the
princess from this bad gift. So he commanded
all the spindles in his kingdom to be burned.

The princess grew up with all the gifts of
the fairies. She was so lovely, sweet, and kind
that everybody loved her.

One day when she was fifteen years old,
she wandered through the castle. She came to

an old tower. She climbed the stairway till she came to a door.

The princess opened the door and went in. There sat an old woman, spinning her flax. This old woman had never heard the king's command.

"Good day, old woman," said the princess. "What are you doing?"

"I am spinning," said the old woman.

"What is the thing that whirls round?" asked the princess. And she took the spindle in her hand. As soon as she touched it, she pricked her finger. The angry fairy's wish had come true.

The princess fell back in a deep sleep. This sleep fell upon the castle. The king and queen fell asleep. The whole court fell asleep. The cook in the kitchen, the horses in the stables, the dogs in the yard, the birds in the trees and the flies on the walls fell asleep. Even the fire on the hearth fell asleep.

A hedge of thorns grew up around the castle. It grew higher and higher every year. At last the whole castle was hidden.

The story of the sleeping princess went all through the country.

Many kings' sons tried to get into the
castle, but the hedge of thorns would not let
them pass. At the end of the hundred years, a
prince came into the country. An old man told
him the story of the sleeping princess.

"I will go through the hedge and find the
beautiful princess," said the prince.

Then the old man told him of the kings'
sons who had tried and who had been caught
in the thorns. "I am not afraid to try," said he.

When the prince came to the hedge of
thorns, it was changed into a hedge of roses. It
parted and let him pass.

In the courtyard he saw the horses and
dogs asleep. In the trees he saw the birds
asleep with their heads under their wings.

He went into the house. There he saw the flies asleep on the wall. He went into the hall. There he saw the queen and the king asleep on the throne.

He went on and at last he came to the tower. He opened the door, and there lay the beautiful princess asleep. He kissed her and took her by the hand. She opened her eyes and looked at him with a smile. She arose and he led her to the king.

The queen and the king awoke. The horses in the courtyard got up and shook themselves. The dogs got up and wagged their tails. The birds lifted their heads from under their wings. The flies on the wall began to crawl. And the cook awoke and went to work.

The whole castle was once more awake, and the prince and princess were married and lived happily ever after.

—*Grimm Brothers*

East o' the Sun and West o' the Moon

A long time ago there was a poor woodman who had many children. They were all pretty, but the youngest daughter was the prettiest of them all.

One cold winter night they sat around the fire. All at once they heard three taps at the door. The woodman went to the door and there stood a great White Bear.

"Good evening to you," said the bear.

"The same to you," said the woodman.

"If you will give me your youngest lassie, I will make you rich," said the bear.

"No, I cannot give her to you," said the woodman.

"Well," said the bear, "I will come back next week."

The next week there came three taps.

This time the lassie went to the door. There stood the White Bear. "Will you go with me?" said the bear. The lassie said she would. So she got on his back and off they went.

When they had gone a bit of the way the White Bear said, "Are you afraid?"

"No," said the lassie.

They rode a long, long way. At last they came to a great hill. The White Bear gave a knock. A door opened and they went into a castle. The rooms were all lighted up and they shone with silver and gold.

The White Bear gave the lassie a bell and said, "Ring this bell whenever you want

anything." And he went away.

When it was dark a man came in. It was the White Bear changed into a man, and he came every night.

One day the lassie found a bit of candle. That night when the man came she lighted it. The light shone on his face and she saw the handsomest prince in the world. She stooped to look at him and three drops of tallow fell on his coat.

"What have you done?" he cried. "You have brought us bad luck. Now I must go away. I must go to the castle East o' the Sun and West o' the Moon. There I must marry the Princess with a nose three ells long. The old witch who lives there has made me a White Bear by day and a man by night. Now I must go away because you have seen me."

The lassie wept, but go he must. Then she asked if she might go with him.

No, she could not go.

"Tell me the way, then," she said, "and I will find you."

"There is no way to that place," he said. "It is East o' the Sun and West o' the Moon."

Next morning when the lassie awoke the.

White Bear was gone. She cried and rubbed her eyes. Then she set out and walked and walked.

At last she came to the East Wind.

"Can you tell me the way to the Castle East o' the Sun and West o' the Moon?" she said. "I want the Prince who is to marry the Princess with a nose three ells long."

"I have heard of him," said the East Wind. "What do you know about him? Maybe you are the lassie who ought to marry him."

Yes, she was the lassie.

"Well, get on my back, and I will carry you to my brother, the West Wind. Maybe he knows the way." So she got on his back and away they went. At last they came to the West Wind.

The East Wind said, "This is the lassie who ought to marry the Prince that lives in the Castle East o' the Sun and West o' the Moon. Can you tell her the way?"

"I have never been so far," said the West Wind. "But get on my back and I will take you to my brother, the South Wind. Maybe he knows the way."

She got on his back and away they went to the South Wind.

The West Wind said, "Do you know the way to the Castle East o' the Sun and West o' the Moon? This is the lassie who ought to marry the Prince that lives there."

"I do not know the way," said the South Wind. "But get on my back. I'll take you to my brother, the North Wind. If he does not know, no one in the world knows."

She got on his back and away they went. At last they came to the North Wind.

"What do you want?" he roared.

The South Wind said, "Here is the lassie who ought to marry the Prince that lives in the Castle East o' the Sun and West o' the Moon. Can you tell her the way?"

"Yes, I know the way. I was there once, and I was so tired that I could not blow a puff for many days. It is a long way from here. But if the lassie wants to go, I will take her there."

So the North Wind puffed himself up and blew himself out and made himself big and stout. The lassie got on his back and off they went.

They went over forests and rivers. They

went over land and sea. On and on they blew. No one knows how far they went.

The North Wind got so tired he could hardly bring out a puff, and his wings drooped and drooped. At last he sank so low that the waves dashed over his heels.

"Are you afraid?" asked he. No, she was not afraid.

At last they came to the land East o' the Sun and West o' the Moon. The North Wind placed the lassie upon the shore near the castle. He was so weak and worn out that he had to rest many days.

The next morning the Prince saw the lassie and she told him the whole story.

"You have come in time," said the Prince,

"I shall not marry Princess Longnose. You shall set me free."

The next day the Prince said, "My wedding coat has three drops of tallow on it. I shall marry the woman who can wash them out."

The Princess with the long nose began to wash. But the more she rubbed the bigger the spots grew.

"Let me try," said the old witch. She rubbed and rubbed, but the spots grew bigger and blacker.

Then all the other trolls began to wash. But the spots got larger and blacker.

"You cannot wash," said the Prince. "A

lassie sits outside who can wash better.

"Come in lassie," shouted the Prince, and in she came. "Can you wash out the spots on the coat, lassie?" he asked.

"I will try," she said. So she dipped the coat into the water and it became white as snow.

"Yes, you are the lassie for me," said the Prince.

Then the old witch flew into a rage and burst. The Princess with the long nose flew into a rage and burst. And the whole pack of trolls burst. At least they have never been heard of since.

The Prince and Princess were set free. So they flitted away from the Castle East o' the Sun and West o' the Moon.

—*Norse Fairy Tale*

Little Maia

Once a fairy planted a little seed in a flower pot. A beautiful flower grew up. It had red and gold petals like a tulip. In it lived a little maiden called Tiny.

A leaf floated on a pond near by. The little maiden made a boat of it. And, with the oars made of horse hairs, she rowed and sang all day long.

Tiny's cradle was a walnut shell with a rose leaf for a cover. One night she lay asleep in her pretty cradle. A toad hopped by and saw her.

"She will make a pretty playmate for my son," said the toad. So he took up the walnut shell and jumped into the garden with it.

When the little toad saw Tiny, he said, "Croak, croak, croak."

The old toad put Tiny on a water leaf in the stream. The little fishes gnawed the stem and it floated away.

The birds in the bushes saw Tiny and sang sweet songs as she sailed by.

A white butterfly flew around her and lighted on the leaf. Away it sailed faster than before.

A beetle flew by and saw the little maiden. He took her in his claws and flew away and left her on a daisy.

That summer Tiny lived in the great woods. She made a bed of grass and hung it under a broad leaf. She ate the honey from the flowers and drank the dew from the leaves.

Then came the long cold winter. The trees and the flowers shed their leaves and all the birds flew away. It began to snow and the poor little maiden was nearly frozen. She wandered into a big cornfield and came to the home of a field mouse. This mouse lived in a hole under the ground.

"You poor little creature," said the field

mouse, "come into my warm room and dine with me."

The field mouse was pleased with Tiny, so she said, "You may stay with me all winter. But you must tell me stories and keep my room clean."

Soon a mole came to visit them. He wore a black velvet coat and the field mouse said to Tiny, "The mole is rich, and he has a big house and plenty of corn. But he is blind, and has never seen the flowers nor the sunshine. So you must tell him your prettiest stories."

Then Tiny sang,
"Lady bird, lady bird, fly away home,
Your house is on fire, your children will
  burn."

The mole had dug a long passage under the ground, and they took many walks in it.

One day the mole pushed his nose through the earth and the light shone in. There in the passage lay a little swallow, with his head under his wing.

Tiny bent down and stroked the little bird. "He sang for me last summer," she said.

That night Tiny wove a cover of hay and

spread it over the bird.

"Farewell, little bird, "she said, "I will remember your pretty songs."

When the bird became warm, he opened his eyes and said, "Thank you, little maiden, for my warm cover. Soon my wing will be well and I shall fly away."

"Oh," said Tiny, "it is so cold. It snows and freezes. Stay in your warm bed and I will take care of you."

Tiny brought him water in a flower. She cared for him all winter.

In the spring he asked her to fly away with him. "You can sit on my back," he said, "and we will fly away into the green woods."

"No, I cannot go," said Tiny, "the field mouse would be sad."

"Farewell, then," said the swallow and he flew out into the sunshine.

All summer the little maiden was sad. She did not want to live under ground all the time.

One morning in the fall she walked out into the sunshine.

"Good morning, bright sun," she said. "Greet the dear swallow for me, if you see him."

"Tweet-tweet! tweet-tweet!" sang the swallow over her head. He was glad to see her again.

Tiny said, "I do not want to live under ground. I want to live in the sunshine with the birds and the flowers."

"Come with me, little maiden," said the swallow. "Winter will soon be here and I shall fly away to a warm country. There the sun shines, the flowers bloom and the birds sing."

"I will go with you," said Tiny. So she

seated herself on his back, and away they flew over land and sea.

At last they came to a blue lake. Under the green trees stood a palace of white marble. The pillars were covered with vines, and at the top were many birds' nests.

The swallow flew down and placed Tiny on a flower. She looked in and saw a little man in the flower. He had wings and he wore a gold crown on his head. He was the king of the flowers.

Tiny was the prettiest little maiden he had ever seen. He asked her to be queen of the flowers.

And he took off his golden crown and put it on her head.

"I shall like to be queen of the flowers," said Tiny.

Then every flower opened, and out of each came a little lord and lady. Each one brought the little queen presents. The best gift was a pair of beautiful wings. Then Tiny could fly from flower to flower. The swallow sang a sweet song to them and everybody was happy.

The King said, "You shall be Queen of the Spring, and you shall be called Maia."

·And so she is called Maia to this very day.

—*Hans Christian Andersen*

Hansel and Gretel

Scene I

Hansel: I wish mother would come home.
I am so hungry. I wish I had
something nice to eat.

Gretel: Now don't look so cross, and I
will tell you a secret.

Hansel: Is it something good to eat?

Gretel: Yes, see the milk in this jug.
When mother comes home she
will make us a pudding.

Hansel: How thick the cream is! Let us
taste it.

Gretel: You are a greedy boy. Go back to work. Mother will soon be home.

Hansel: Work again? Not I! I am tired of making brooms. Let us have some fun.

Gretel: And I am tired of knitting.
Brother, come and dance with
  me;
Both my hands I offer thee;
Right foot first, Left foot then,
Round about and back again.

Hansel: I would dance, but don't know
  how,
When to jump, and when to bow.
Show me what I ought to do,
So that I may dance like you.

Gretel: With your foot you tap, tap, tap;
With your hands you clap, clap,
  clap;
Right foot first, Left foot then,
Round about and back again.

Hansel: With your hands you clap, clap,
  clap;
With your foot you tap, tap, tap;
Right foot first, Left foot then,
Round about and back again.

Gretel: Try again and I can see,
Hansel will soon dance like me.

[Mother enters.]

Hansel: Here comes mother!

Mother: What is all this noise about?
Come, children, show me your
work. How many brooms have
you made, Hansel? Is your
stocking finished, Gretel?

Hansel: We have been playing, mother.

Mother: You lazy children! I must get
my stick and make your fingers
tingle.

[She reaches for the stick and upsets the jug of milk]

Hansel: No pudding? And I am so
hungry. Oh! oh!

Mother: And I have sold nothing today, so
we can have no supper.

Hansel: We can go to the woods and get
strawberries. Come, Gretel.

[Father enters.]

Father: Well, mother, what have we to
eat today? I am so hungry.

Mother: We have nothing to eat. I had no luck today, and I spilt the milk, so we can have no pudding.

Father: Cheer up, mother. I have had luck today. Look in my basket and see what I bought at the market.

Mother: What do I see? Ham and eggs, bread and butter, turnips and onions, and nearly a half pound of tea.

Father: Where are the children?

Mother: They have gone to the woods for strawberries.

Father: Mother, do you not know an old witch lives there?

Mother: What do you say, father?

Father: An old witch lives in the woods.
And at midnight when nobody
    knows,
Away to the witches' dance she
    goes;
Up the chimney they fly,
On a broomstick they hie;

Father: Through the midnight air
They gallop and tear.

Mother: Does she harm little children?

Father: They say,
In the oven red-hot,
She pops the whole lot;
And she shuts the lid down,
Till they are done brown.
Then they are gingerbread
children.

Mother: What does she do with the
gingerbread children?

Father: She serves them for dinner.

Mother: Oh! what shall we do?

Father: We must go to the woods and
find the children.

SCENE II

Hansel: My basket is full of berries. Won't mother be pleased? Here is a large berry. I will give it to you, Gretel.

Gretel: That was good. You shall have one, too. Here is a large one for you.

Hansel: You shall have another.

Gretel: And you shall have another.

Hansel: You shall have another and I shall have another, and you shall have another.

Gretel: Oh, what have we done? All the berries are gone. What will mother say?

Hansel: Let us get more berries.

Gretel: I cannot find any. It is getting
dark. Let us go home.

Hansel: I cannot find the way.

Gretel: Do you hear that noise, Hansel?
I am afraid.

Hansel: I am a boy. I am not afraid.

Gretel: What is that over there?

Hansel: It is only the stump of a tree.

Gretel: But it is making faces at me.

Hansel: I will make faces at it.

Gretel: It is coming this way, Hansel.

Hansel: I will call. Who is there?

Echo: You there!

Gretel: Did you hear that? I am afraid.

Hansel: I will take care of you, Gretel.

Gretel: There stands a little man.
Say, who can he be,
Standing by himself under that
tree?

Gretel: His hair is gold, and his cheeks
are red.
He wears a little cap on his head.
Who can the little man be?

Sandman: I shut the children's peepers,
sh!
I guard the little sleepers, sh!
For dearly do I love them, sh!
And gladly watch above them,
sh!
And with my bag of sand,
By every little child I stand,
Till their eyelids close,
Then sleep, children, sleep.
Sh! sh! sh!

Gretel: Let us say our prayers, and the
angels will watch over us.
When at night I go to sleep,
Fourteen angels watch do keep:
Two at my head, two at my feet;
Two at my right hand,
Two on my left hand;
Two to cover me,
Two to show me
The way to Heaven.

SCENE III

Dewman: Ding! dong! ding! dong!
With the light of day,
I chase the night away.
Fresh dew around I shake,
And hill and dale awake.
Awake, children, awake.

Gretel: Where am I? How did I get here?
Wake up, Hansel. The sun is
shining and I hear the birds
singing.

Hansel: I am awake. I hear the birds.
What place is this? Do you see that
little house? It is made

of chocolate creams, and the roof is
sugar and raisins. And all around
it is a gingerbread fence. It must
be good to eat. Come, let us take a
nibble.

Gretel: Oh, no! We do not know who lives
there. But it does smell good.
Let us break off a little piece and
nibble like two little mice.

Witch: Nibble, nibble, mousekin,
Who nibbles at my housekin? Who
nibbles at my housekin?

Gretel: Do you hear that?

Hansel: It was only the wind.

Witch: So you have come to visit me?
That is sweet.
Let me see?

Hansel: Who are you? Let me go!

Witch: I am the witch, as you see,
I love little children.
Come with me.

Hansel: Go away, you are so ugly. Come,
sister, let us run away.

Witch: Hocus, pocus, come with me.
Hocus, pocus, just we three. Now,
Gretel, be good and wise, While
Hansel grows fat and nice.
And bring some cakes and meat,
For Hansel wants more to eat.

[The Witch puts Hansel in a cage, then opens the
oven door.]

Yes, Gretel mine,
Now I will dine.
She is so tender, plump, and good,
Just the thing for witch's food.
When in the oven she does peep,
Quickly behind her I will creep.
One little push, bang!
Shut the door, clang!
When from the oven I take her,
She will be a cake from the baker,
By magic fire made red,
Changed into gingerbread.

SCENE IV

Witch: Hop, hop, hop, hop, Gallop, lop,
    lop.
My broomstick nag, Come, do
    not lag.
At dawn of day, I ride away.
I am here and there,
I am everywhere!
At midnight, when no one can
    know,
To the witches' dance I go.
One, two, three, four, five, six,
All of these are witches' tricks.

Witch: Come, my little mankin,
Show me your thumbkin.
Oh, you are a skinny one;
I shall wait a while to dine.
Come, Gretel mine,
Peep in the oven, be steady,
See if Hansel's cake is ready.

Hansel: Sister dear, have a care.

Gretel: I do not know how to peep into the
    oven.

Witch: Just stand on tiptoe,
And bend your head low.

Gretel: You will have to show me how.

Witch: Do as I say. It is only play.

Gretel: Hocus, pocus, elder bush,
Ugly body, in we push.
One little push, bang!
Shut the door, clang!
When from the oven we take her,

Gretel: She will be a cake from the baker,
By magic fire made red,
Changed into gingerbread.

Hansel: The old witch is caught in her own trap. She will soon be made into gingerbread. Then the house will be ours. Come, let us eat our fill. Hurrah!

Gretel: Oh, see the gingerbread children.

Hansel: Who are you? Your eyes are shut, still you are singing.

Gingerbread children: Oh touch us with the wand, that we may wake.

Gretel: Hocus, pocus, one, two, three; Hocus, pocus, now you can see.

Gingerbread children: Now we are free. We will dance and sing And shout for glee! Come let us form a ring, And join hands while we sing.

[Father and Mother enter.]

Hansel: Here come father and mother.

Mother: Our children are safe.

Father: Where is the old witch?

Gingerbread children: Here she is. She is gingerbread now and we are free.

Father: She is caught in her own trap.

Gretel: Let us all join hands and sing.
With your feet you tap, tap, tap;
With your hands you clap, clap,
    clap;
Right foot first, Left foot then,
Round about and back again.

—Adapted from the text by Adelheid Wette

PETER PAN

Peter Pan looked out of the window. He
saw the trees in the Gardens. He forgot he
was a little boy in a nightgown. He thought
he was a bird and could fly. So he flew out
of the window over the houses into the
Gardens. Then he settled into the grass by the
Serpentine.

The Serpentine is a long blue lake. It has a
drowned forest in it. If you look over the edge
you can see the trees growing upside down.
And at night there are drowned stars in it.

When Peter saw the water he wanted a
drink. He flew to the pond and dipped his nose
into the water. He thought it was a bill, but it
was only his nose. So not much water came up.

He tried again and this time he fell flop into the water.

If he had been a bird he would have spread his feathers to dry. But Peter could not think what to do. So he lay down and went to sleep.

When he awoke his nose was stuffy. He did not know what to do, so he lay down on his back and kicked. It was Lock-out-Time in the Gardens. Lock-out-Time is when the gates are locked and the fairies come out to play. There were fairies all about.

Some were milking the cows, some were getting breakfast, and some were walking on the garden path.

"I will ask the fairies what to do," said Peter. So he flew to a fairy on a seat. But the fairy hopped behind a tulip and hid. Then he flew to the fairies on the garden walk, but they ran away. Some fairy workmen left their tools and ran. A fairy milkmaid turned her pail upside down and hid in it.

Soon the Gardens were in an uproar. Crowds of fairies were running this way and that way. Lights were put out and doors were locked.

A rub-a-dub-dub of drums was heard. The

fairy soldiers had been called out. Peter heard them say, "A human is in the Gardens after Lock-out-Time."

Peter did not know that he was a human. So when all the fairies ran from him he sat down and cried.

Peter's nose got stuffier and stuffier. He said, "I will ask the birds what to do." So he flew to the birds' island.

The birds' island is in the Serpentine outside the Gardens. The birds were all asleep except old Solomon Caw. Peter told old Solomon about his nose, and Solomon told him that he was a human. But Peter could not believe it.

Old Solomon said, "Look at your night-gown, if you do not believe me. How many of your toes are thumbs? Ruffle your feathers." But he could not do it. So now Peter knew that he was not a bird.

"I shall go back to the Gardens," said he.

"Good bye," said Solomon. "Why don't you go?"

"I cannot fly," said Peter.

"Poor little Half-and-Half," said Solomon, "you can never fly again. You must live on this island with the birds."

"And never go to the Gardens?" asked Peter.

"How can you get there?" asked old Solomon Caw. "But you can live here with us and I will teach you the ways of the birds."

"Then shall I be a bird?" asked Peter.

"No," said Solomon.

"Shall I be a human?" said Peter.

"No," said Solomon.

"What shall I be, then?" asked Peter.

"You will be a Betwixt-and-Between." So Peter lived on the island with the birds. He helped them build their nests. He took care of the sick ones. He dug worms for the young ones.

But he would not eat the worms and insects. So the birds brought him crumbs from the Gardens. Then they flew about to see him eat with his hands.

Peter learned all the ways of the birds. He could see the grass grow. He could hear the insects inside the tree trunks. And he could tell an east wind from a west wind by the smell.

Old Solomon taught Peter to have a glad heart. Peter was so happy he wanted to sing all the time.

So he made a pipe of reeds. He put into it a handful of moonshine. He put in the rippling of the waters. He put in the whispering of the trees, the nodding of the flowers, and the sighing of the winds.

He sat on the shore and played for the birds. They would say, "Is that Peter Pan playing, or is it the wind?"

Sometimes Peter was sad. Then his music was sad. He was sad because he wanted to go to the Gardens. He wanted to play like other boys.

He tried to think of a way to get to the

Gardens. One day he said, "I could swim if someone would teach me." The ducks said they would teach him. But ducks do not know how to teach.

They would say to Peter, "Sit down on the water and kick out as we do." Peter sat down on the water, but he sank before he could kick out.

Then one day a kite fell on the island. The birds showed Peter how to fly it. Then Peter said, "Now I can get to the Gardens. I will hang on the tail of the kite, and the birds .will take me over." So Peter hung on the tail of the kite, and a hundred birds flew off with it.

But they had not gone far when the kite broke, and Peter fell into the water. He would have drowned, but a swan carried him back to the island.

Then Peter thought of another way. He said, "If I had a nest big enough, it would make a good boat. A thrush's nest would be best, for it is lined with mud and will not leak."

He told the birds about it. So they went to work. They worked a long time, till they had made a nest big enough for Peter. Then Peter made a sail of his nightgown.

One night, when the moon was shining and the birds were all asleep, Peter got into his boat and sailed away. He sailed straight to the Gardens. There he found a crowd of fairies on the shore. They would not let him land.

Peter said, "I am a friend; I came from the birds' island."

They answered, "It is past Lock-out-Time. Be off." But Peter jumped out of his boat right into the crowd of fairies.

They took him to the fairy queen. When she saw Peter she said, "You may stay in the Gardens after Lock-out-Time." So Peter lived in the Gardens after Lock-out-Time. The fairies told him how little boys play. They know, for they are in the Gardens all day, but no one can see them. If anyone looks at them they run away. If they cannot run away they stand still and pretend they are flowers.

There are many fairies in the world. The first time a baby laughs, the laugh slips away and becomes a fairy.

Fairies love music, so Peter played his pipe for them. They love to dance, too. They danced in a fairy ring, and Peter sat on a toadstool in the middle of the ring and played. They called it the Peter Pan Band.

The fairy queen was delighted with his music, so he played for her every day.

One day she said, "Peter, I will give you the wish of your heart."

The fairies gathered around Peter to hear the wish of his heart.

"I wish to go home to my mother," said Peter.

The fairies did not want Peter to go. So they said, "That is such a little wish, make a big one."

"I will make two little ones," said Peter, "instead of one big one. I wish to go home to my mother. Then I wish to come back when I want to."

This pleased the fairy queen, and she gave him the power to fly.

So Peter flew away over the trees and housetops. When he reached home he found the window wide open. He flew in and sat at the foot of the bed. There lay his mother sound asleep. She looked very beautiful, but she looked sad.

"Oh, mother," said Peter, "if you only knew who was sitting on the foot of your bed." Then he flew to the drawer. There were all his pretty clothes.

But he could not remember how to put them on. Then he heard his mother say,

"Peter," in her sleep. It sounded so sad. Then he flew back to the foot of her bed and played a sad tune on his pipe.

Then he looked at his mother and said, "I love my mother and I would like to stay with her, but I did not say good bye to the birds. I will go and say 'Good bye,' then I will come back to her."

He wanted to kiss his mother good bye, but he was afraid he would wake her. So he played a kiss on his pipe and flew away.

He played for the fairies, helped the birds, and sailed his boat. So it was a long time before he asked to go back to his mother.

But one day he said to the fairy queen, "I want to go to my mother for always." The queen said he could go.

When Peter reached home this time the window was shut. He called, "Mother, mother," but she did not answer. He went to the window and peeped in.

There lay his mother with another little baby boy on her arm. She looked so happy that Peter said, "Now, I can go back to the fairies and birds." So he flew away to the Gardens.

Now Peter lives with the birds and fairies. He helps the birds build their nests. He gets worms for the young ones. He sails his boat and plays for the fairies. And he rides around on a little goat to find little children who have strayed among the fairies.

—*Adapted from James M. Barrie's*
"Little White Bird"

GROUP OF POEMS

THE NEW MOON

Dear mother, how pretty
    The moon looks to-night!
She was never so cunning before;
    Her two little horns
    Are so sharp and so bright,
I hope she'll not grow any more.

If I were up there
    With you and my friends,
I'd rock in it nicely, you'd see;
    I'd sit in the middle
    And hold by both ends;
Oh, what a bright cradle 'twould be!

I would call to the stars
    To keep out of the way,
Lest we should rock over their toes;
    And then I would rock
    Till the dawn of the day,
And see where the pretty moon goes.

And there we would stay
    In the beautiful skies,
And through the bright clouds we would
      roam;
    We would see the sun set,
    And see the sun rise,
And on the next rainbow come home.

—Eliza Follen

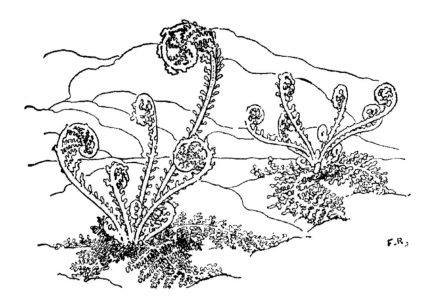

The Ferns

Oh, what shall we do
 The long winter through?
The baby ferns cried
 When the mother fern died.

The wind whistled bleak,
 And the woodland was drear,
And on each baby cheek
 There glistened a tear.

Then down from the clouds
 Like a flutter of wings,

There came a whole crowd
    Of tiny white things.

They trooped in a heap,
    Where the baby ferns lay,
And put them to sleep,
    That bleak, bitter day.

Tucked under the snow
    In their little brown hoods,
Not a thing will they know,
    Those "Babes in the Woods."

Till some day in spring,
    When the bobolinks sing,
They will open their eyes
    To the bluest of skies.

—Mrs. S.C. Cornwall

SLEEP, BABY, SLEEP!

Sleep, baby, sleep!
Thy father watches his sheep;
Thy mother is shaking the dreamland tree,
And down comes a little dream on thee.
Sleep, baby, sleep!

Sleep, baby, sleep!
The large stars are the sheep;
The little stars are the lambs, I guess;
The gentle moon is the shepherdess.
Sleep, baby, sleep!

—From the German

THE LOST DOLL

I once had a sweet little doll, dears,
    The prettiest doll in the world;
Her cheeks were so red and white, dears,
    And her hair was beautifully curled.

But I lost my poor little doll, dears,
    As I played on the heath one day;
And I cried for her more than a week, dears,
    And I never could find where she lay.

I found my poor little doll, dears,
    As I played on the heath one day;
Folks say she is very much changed, dears,
    For her paint is all washed away.

And her arms trodden off by the cows, dears,
    And her hair not the least bit curled;
Yet for old sake's sake she is still, dears,
    The prettiest doll in the world.

—Charles Kingsley

THE LITTLE ELF

I met a little Elf-man, once,
    Down where the lilies blow.
I asked him why he was so small
    And why he didn't grow.

He slightly frowned, and with his eye
    He looked me through and through.
"I'm quite as big for me," said he,
    "As you are big for you."

                —*John Kendrick Bangs*

AN ELFIN FAIR

O, I would that I were
    An Elfin fair,
    An Elfin fair:
I'd ride upon moonbeams
    And sport in the air,
    Sport in the air.

                —*Bjørnstjerne Bjørnson*

FAIRY FOLK

Up the airy mountain
    Down the rushy glen,
We dare not go a-hunting,
    For fear of little men;

Wee folk, good folk,
    Trooping all together
Green jacket, red cap,
    And white owl's feather.

Down along the rock shore
    Some make their home;

They live on crispy pancakes
    Of yellow seafoam.

High on the hilltop
    The old king sits;
He is now so old and gray,
    He's nigh lost his wits.

Up the airy mountain,
    Down the rushy glen,
We daren't go a-hunting
    For fear of little men;

Wee folk, good folk,
    Trooping all together;
Green jacket, red cap,
    And white owl feather.

           —*William Allingham*

WORD LIST

This list includes words in the READING-LITERATURE SECOND READER, except those already used in an earlier book of this series and a few that present no difficulty in spelling, pronunciation, or meaning.

THE WIND AND THE SUN PAGE 1

quarrel	closer	tried	madam
move	harder	pebbles	glossy
summer	warmer	drowned	snapped
cover	unbuttoned	wanted	foolish
cloak	thirsty	piece	flatter
cloud	pitcher	mouth	

THE GOOSE THAT LAID THE GOLDEN EGG PAGE 5

egg	race	plodded	village
greedy	tortoise	animals	clubs
wrung	goal	timid	really
content	fixed	anything	killed
golden	bound	shepherd	
beaten	nap	kept	

THE JAY AND THE PEACOCK PAGE 9

peacocks	jay	ashamed

THE FOX AND THE STORK PAGE 11

moonlight	harm	served	long-necked
lion	invited	tongue	jar
beast			

The Man, the Boy, and the Donkey Page 12

market	donkey	pair	loose
walking	shame	pole	nobody
beside	lazy		

The Lion and the Mouse Page 14

caught	trap	groaned	gnawed

Come Out to Play Page 15

leave	whoop	halfpenny pudding
playfellows	ladder	

I Saw a Ship a-Sailing Page 16

a-sailing	cabin	masts	captain
laden	sails	twenty	packet
comfits	silk	chains	

Who Killed Cock Robin? Page 17

shroud	parson	torch	mourner
beetle	Rook	Linnet	thrush
needle	clerk	fetch	bull
grave	Lark	minute	pull
spade	Kite	chief	farewell
shovel			

There Was a Little Man Page 20

bullets	Joan	drake	mark
lead	roast		

The Fir Tree Page 21

watered	spread	everything	trembled
roots	stately	candies	shouted
sunshine	toys	wax	

THE DISCONTENTED PINE TREE PAGE 25

music	sparkle	prettiest	shivered
needles			

BOOTS AND HIS BROTHERS PAGE 28

Peter	kingdom	wallet	woodpecker
Paul	softer	steep	walnut
Boots	hewing	digging	trickling
youngest	hacking	delving	chip
palace	woodcutter	stooped	frighten
daughter	waiting		

THE ELVES AND THE SHOEMAKER PAGE 34

elves	paid	midnight	trousers
early	price	skipping	danced
stitch	enough	hammer	

CINDERELLA PAGE 37

dishes	coach	chose	banquet
scrubbed	watched	jolly	quarter
stairs	godmother	lizards	twelve
cinders	sight	footmen	hurried
Cinderella	appeared	slippers	thanked
haughty	pumpkin	remember	lovely
dresses	scooped	return	forget
clothes	touched	ragged	messenger
gowns	gilded	princess	court
ribbons	mousetrap	seat	married
laces	pantry	honor	
jewels	coachman		

Hans in Luck Page 45

Hans	ditch	eight	grinder
luck	bargain	feel	whirling
wages	noon	whoever	wheel
handkerchiefs	squeeze	wipe	scissors
trotting	matter	mayor	trade
hurts	sausage	grew	pocket
change	taste	risk	grindstone
click	showed	pillow	
gee	stuffing		

A Linnet Page 53

bough	doubt	frosty

What is Pink? Page 54

pink	barley	pears	violet
fountains	swan	yellow	twilight
brink	float	mellow	orange
poppy's			

In the Meadow Page 55

bluebells	buttercups

Daisies Page 55

daisies	bright-eyed	blades	between
buttercups			

A Diamond or a Coal Page 56

coal	clumsy	beneath	freeze

An Emerald is as Green as Grass Page 56

emerald	sapphire	brilliant	opal
ruby	shines	desire	fiery
red	flint		

The Peach Tree Page 57

peach	score	rosiest	downiest
southern	bloom	grandmamma	
basked	biggest		

The Wind Page 58

neither passing

Boats Sail on the Rivers Page 59

heaven overtops

The Birthday Gift Page 60

birthday gifts

The Lambkins Page 60

keen	careful	nestlings	anew
nestle	ewe	nightly	

The Queen Bee Page 61

smothered	spell	heap	lake
locks	hundred	task	dived
pearls	piled	key	sugar
thousand	saving	bottom	syrup
magic			

The Brave Tin Soldier Page 66

tin	paper	war	goblin
clapping	around	parties	meant
twenty-five	scarf	nutcracker	suddenly
exactly	stretched	somersaults	straight
alike	mate	pencils	musket
except	grand	tattled	newspaper
enough	snuffbox	firm	bravely
finish	visiting	bounce	shouldered

THE BRAVE TIN SOLDIER continued

gutter	tighter	jerked	melting
ahead	roaring	playroom	flashed
channel	whirled	wondered	flame
passport	waterfall		

THE SISTER OF THE SUN PAGE 72

Lars	agree	giant	blinded
gardener	peasant	happened	join
quiet	friendly	mess	feasting
behaved	smelled	shipped	prove
arrows	tucked	whenever	worthy
playground	worse	chase	performed
sticking	cackle		

WHY THE SEA IS SALT PAGE 80

whatever	begged	Eve	twisted
chopping	outbid	haymaking	seashore
evening	obeyed	herring	offer
rapped	neighbors	pottage	

THE FLYING SHIP PAGE 87

Czar	shooting	won	oxen
blessing	shot	welcome	tons
somewhere	sack	living	twenty
knapsack	mouthful	command	barrels
whirring	Drinker	end	trick
untie	becomes	returned	bathroom
halfway	bundle	snoring	stove
swift	army	roasted	raise

The Flying Ship continued

sadly	bugles	terror	robes
became	presented	royal	wedding

Fairy Land Page 100

alone	clover	wander	parcels
pleasant	rain-pools	marching	climber
land	leaflet	carrying	sleepy-head
afar	drifting		

The Swing Page 102

swing	cattle	countryside

Rain Page 103

raining	umbrellas

Singing Page 103

speckled	Japan	Spain	organ

At the Seaside Page 104

seaside	sandy	empty	every
wooden			

Farewell to the Farm Page 104

mounting	meadow-gates	evermore	crack
chorus	pump	hayloft	whip
lawn	stable	cling	woody

Time to Rise Page 105

window-sill	cocked

Whole Duty of Children Page 105

mannerly	least

Looking Forward Page 106

estate	meddle

Bed in Summer Page 107

candlelight hopping grown-up

Where Go the Boats? Page 108

forever either a-floating a-boating

My Shadow Page 109

heels proper notion coward
funniest sometimes ought nursie
india-rubber

Sleeping Beauty Page 111

kindness protect thorns wagged
eleven stairway courtyard crawl
stepped pricked themselves whole
spindles

East o' the Sun and West o' the Moon Page 116

woodman ells placed blacker
lassie maybe longnose rage
knock dropped tallow burst
wept weak wash pack
rubbed worn

Little Maia Page 124

planted cornfield passage marble
petals creature stroked pillars
tulip dine wove vines
shell clean greet Maia
playmate mole tweet-tweet
croak velvet

HANSEL AND GRETEL PAGE 131

Hansel	today	eyelids	tender
Gretel	strawberries	prayers	plump
secret	split	fourteen	creep
thick	onions	angels	clang
cream	pound	ding	bang
greedy	tea	dong	cake
making	witch	dales	baker
knitting	hie	chocolate	nag
offer	broomstick	raisins	lag
right	gallop	nibble	mankin
left	stump	mousekin	thumpkin
stocking	standing	housekin	skinny
tingle	cheeks	ugly	tiptoe
upset	peepers	hocus	elder
sold	sleepers	pocus	hurrah

PETER PAN PAGE 146

nightgown	uproar	tree	sighing
Serpentine	rub-a-dub-dub	trunks	sank
dipped	human	Betwixt-and-between	lined
stuffy	stuffier	pipe	leak
lock-out-time	Solomon	reeds	pretend
locked	ruffle	handful	delighted
milking	teach	moonshine	gathered
breakfast	island	rippling	housetops
workman	worms	whispering	answer
milkmaid	insects	nodding	strayed

THE NEW MOON PAGE 157

cunning   nicely   roam   rainbow

THE FERNS PAGE 159

ferns   woodland flutter   hoods
whistled   drear   trooped   bobolinks
bleak   glistened bitter

SLEEP, BABY, SLEEP PAGE 161

dreamland guess   shepherdess

THE LOST DOLL PAGE 162

beautifully curled   paint   sake
           heath   trodden

THE LITTLE ELF PAGE 163

elfman

THE ELFIN FAIR PAGE 163

no new words

FAIRY FOLK PAGE 164

airy   owl's   hilltop   wits
rushy   crispy   nigh   daren't
glen   seafoam

PHONIC SERIES

1	6	10	14	17
r ed	s ob	w ill	m et	t in
b ed	b ob	t ill	s et	s in
f ed	r ob	b ill	g et	b in
l ed	c ob	s ill	b et	f in
N ed	f ob	f ill	l et	d in
	j ob	r ill	j et	p in
2	m ob	k ill	n et	k in
h en		h ill	p et	
d en	**7**	m ill		**18**
p en	p ig	p ill	**15**	p up
m en	b ig		r un	c up
B en	r ig	**11**	d un	s up
	d ig	d og	s un	
3	j ig	b og	n un	**19**
c at	w ig	h og	g un	r ap
f at		c og	b un	c ap
h at	**8**	f og	f un	g ap
r at	ox	j og		l ap
m at	b ox		**16**	n ap
s at	f ox	**12**	f ed	t ap
		c ut	g ot	m ap
4	**9**	n ut	t an	s ap
c an	it	r ut	h at	
D an	w it	b ut	s at	**20**
f an	s it	h ut	b at	p ad
r an	b it		t en	b ad
p an	p it	**13**	l ed	l ad
	f it	d id		s ad
5	h it	l id		m ad
n ot	m it	b id		h ad
d ot		k id		f ad
g ot		h id		g ad
c ot				
p ot				
j ot				
h ot				

21	**27**	**Review**	**33**	**37**
l eg	r ag	red	b e	g o
p eg	w ag	hen	m e	s o
b eg	b ag	cat	h e	n o
k eg	t ag	can	th e	
	s ag	not	sh e	**38**
22		sob	w e	b ite
l ip	**28**	pig		k ite
t ip	ax	ox	**34**	s ite
d ip	t ax	it	m ake	m ite
r ip	w ax	will	b ake	
h ip		dog	sh ake	**39**
s ip	**29**	cut	c ake	g oat
n ip	c ab	did	t ake	m oat
	t ab	met	f ake	c oat
23		run	r ake	fl oat
m ud	**30**	tin	m ake	b oat
b ud	h im	pup	s ake	
	d im	rap	l ake	**40**
24	r im	pad		c ane
b ug		leg	**35**	p ane
r ug	**31**	lip	b ee	m ane
d ug	f ix	mud	f ee	
p ug	s ix	bug	s ee	**41**
m ug	m ix	tub	l ee	ate
h ug		am	tr ee	d ate
t ug	**32**	rag		r ate
	r od	ax	**36**	f ate
25	G od	cab	t old	m ate
t ub	p od	him	c old	g ate
h ub	h od	fix	b old	l ate
r ub	s od	rod	h old	h ate
	n od		g old	
26			f old	
am			s old	
S am			m old	
h am				
j am				

177

42	**48**	**55**	**61**	**62**
s ame	r ode	c ore	f ire	b ack
t ame	c ode	t ore	w ire	l ack
c ame	m ode	s ore	h ire	p ack
n ame		m ore	t ire	t ack
f ame	**49**	w ore		s ack
l ame	n ote		**Review**	
g ame	c ote	**56**	be	**63**
	d ote	l ope	make	n eck
43	m ote	c ope	bee	d eck
c ape	r ote	d ope	told	
t ape		r ope	go	**64**
	50	m ope	bite	s ick
44	g ale	h ope	goat	k ick
m ade	p ale		cane	t ick
w ade	s ale	**57**	ate	l ick
f ade	t ale	r age	same	p ick
		p age	cape	
45	**51**	c age	made	**65**
h ide	p ole	s age	hide	r ock
w ide	m ole		dime	l ock
b ide	h ole	**58**	fine	
t ide	s ole	b ase	rode	**66**
r ide		c ase	note	d uck
s ide	**52**	v ase	gale	l uck
	t une		pole	b uck
46	J une	**59**	tune	
d ime	pr une	c ave	pure	**67**
t ime	r ule	w ave	mule	s ell
l ime	r ude	g ave	core	N ell
		s ave	lope	t ell
47	**53**	p ave	rage	b ell
f ine	p ure		base	w ell
p ine	c ure	**60**	cave	f ell
d ine		m ile	mile	
n ine	**54**	t ile	fire	
w ine	m ule	p ile		
f ine	m ute	f ile		
l ine				

68	74	Review (cont.)	82	86
p uff	f ist	sell	cr y	D utch
r uff	m ist	puff	cr ape	b otch
c uff	l ist	and	cr ew	n otch
b uff		end	cr ime	p itch
m uff	**75**	bent	cr ate	w itch
	r ust	tint	cr ow	d itch
69	m ust	rest	cr umb	h itch
and	j ust	fist		c atch
h and	d ust	rust	**83**	m atch
s and		camp	gr and	p atch
l and	**76**	bump	gr ave	l atch
b and	c amp	felt	gr ip	h atch
	l amp	gift	gr ill	
70	d amp		gr it	**87**
end		**80**	gr in	m uch
m end	**77**	is	gr ow	s uch
b end	b ump		gr ew	r ich
s end	p ump	h is	gr een	
	j ump	as	gr ound	**88**
71	d ump	h as		sh ape
b ent	l ump	p ins	**84**	sh am
s ent		r ugs	ch ick	sh ell
r ent	**78**	r ose	ch oke	sh elf
w ent	f elt	r ise	ch op	sh ed
t ent	b elt	n ose	ch at	sh ip
	w elt	w ise	ch in	sh ine
72	m elt		ch ase	sh un
t int		**81**	ch ill	sh ut
h int	**79**	wh en	ch ap	sh ot
m int	g ift	wh at	ch afe	sh one
l int	s ift	wh ile		sh ore
	l ift	wh o	**85**	sh ave
73		wh ite	p un ch	sh all
r est	**Review**	wh ole	b en ch	sh ade
v est	back	wh ine	b un ch	sh ake
t est	neck	wh ich	l un ch	
w est	sick	wh ere		
b est	rock	wh ip		
n est	duck			

89	**94**	**96**	**100**	**103**
ash	thr ob	cl od	sp an	scr ap
s ash	thr ift	cl ose	sp ade	scr ub
d ash	thr ill	cl ove	sp in	scr ape
l ash	thr one	cl ock	sp end	scr atch
c ash	thr ash	cl am	sp ill	
m ash	thr ush	cl ap	sp ell	**104**
f ish	thr ive	cl ick	sp ine	sc ore
d ish	thr ust	cl uck	sp ot	sc um
w ish		cl ip	sp oke	sc at
r ush	**Review**	cl ub	sp un	sc amp
	is		sp ite	sc ale
90	when	**97**	sp ike	Sc otch
th ick	cry	fl at	sp ire	
th in	grand	fl ag		**105**
th ump	chick	fl ake	**101**	sk in
	punch	fl ame	br ag	sk im
91	Dutch	fl ash	br an	sk ip
w id th	much	fl ock	br ake	sk iff
t en th	shape	fl op	br ave	sk ill
	ash	fl it	br im	sk ull
92	thick	fl ax	br ick	sk ate
th e	tenth		br ide	sk etch
th en	width	**98**	br ine	
th em	the	gl ad	br oke	**106**
th an	bathe	gl ide	br ush	r isk
th at	throb	gl aze		br isk
th us		gl obe	**102**	t usk
th ese	**95**		cr ab	d usk
th ose	bl ed	**99**	cr ib	h usk
th is	bl ade	pl an	cr ock	m usk
th ine	bl ack	pl ant	cr ack	
	bl ess	pl ate	cr ate	**107**
93	bl ame	pl ush	cr ane	dr op
b athe	bl ot	pl ume	cr amp	dr ag
w ith	bl ock	pl um	cr imp	dr ug
	bl aze	pl ot	cr op	dr ip
	bl unt		cr ust	dr ill
	bl ush		cr ush	dr ift
			cr ept	dr ive

107 (cont.)	110 (cont.)	113	118	Review (cont.)
dr ove	tr od	t aste	sw am	print
dr one	tr uck	p aste	sw im	trap
dr ape		b aste	sw um	strap
dr ess	**111**	w aste	sw ept	stab
dr um	str ap		sw ift	taste
	str ip	**114**	sw ine	lest
108	str ipe	l est		trust
fr et	str ive	cr est	**119**	smell
fr esh	str ict	ch est	tw ist	snap
Fr ench	str ike	bl est	tw ins	swam
fr ill	str ide		tw ine	twist
fr isk	str ide	**115**	tw ig	quench
fr og	str oke	tr ust	tw itch	
fr om	str etch	cr ust		**121**
fr oze		r ust	**120**	y es
fr ame	**112**		qu ench	y et
fr ock	st ab	**116**	qu ick	y ell
	st ep	sm ell	qu ack	
109	st em	sm elt	qu it	**122**
pr int	st ack	sm ile	qu ite	H en ny
pr ide	st and	sm ith	qu ill	m er ry
pr ize	st ate	sm ash	qu ilt	c an dy
pr op	st ump	sm ack		k it ty
pr ose	st ale	sm oke	**Review**	p en ny
pr ess	st ake		bled	s un ny
	st iff	**117**	clod	f un ny
110	st ilt	sn ap	flat	c ar ry
tr ap	st ill	sn ag	glad	j ol ly
tr act	st ick	sn ug	plan	
tr ack	st one	sn ake	span	**123**
tr ash	st ove	sn uff	brag	cr y
tr amp	st op	sn iff	crab	m y
tr ade	st itch	sn ipe	scrap	dr y
tr ip	st ub	sn are	score	sl y
tr im	st uck		skin	sp y
tr ill	st uff		risk	sk y
tr ick	st ore		drop	sh y
tr ot	st ole		fret	fl y
	st ump			wh y
				th y

124	129	135	141	146
aid	t ea	t ear	f eel	d ie
p aid	s ea	n ear	h eel	t ie
br aid	p ea	h ear	p eel	h ie
m aid		cl ear	r eel	l ie
	130		st eel	
125	each	**136**		**147**
ail	p each	east	**142**	t oad
p ail	r each	b east	s een	l oad
h ail	t each	f east	k een	r oad
f ail			gr een	
n ail	**131**	**137**	qu een	**148**
r ail	w eak	eat		oak
s ail	l eak	m eat	**143**	s oak
b ail	p eak	b eat	k eep	cl oak
	sp eak	n eat	st eep	
126	str eak	s eat	d eep	**149**
aim	sn eak	h eat	p eep	oat
m aim	squ eak		sh eep	g oat
cl aim		**138**	sl eep	c oat
	132	pl ea se	cr eep	fl oat
127	h eal	t ea se	sw eep	thr oat
r ain	s eal	ea sy		
tr ain	st eal		**144**	**150**
br ain	m eal	**139**	f eet	t oast
gr ain	squ eal	s eed	m eet	r oast
str ain		f eed	b eet	c oast
p ain	**133**	n eed	sw eet	b oast
pl ain	dr eam	d eed	gr eet	
ch ain	t eam	w eed	str eet	**151**
	str eam	bl eed		oar
128	st eam		**145**	r oar
h ay		**140**	fr eeze	s oar
p ay	**134**	w eek	sn eeze	h oar se
s ay	b ean	ch eek	br eeze	c oar se
w ay	m ean	cr eek	squ eeze	b oar d
m ay	l ean			
pl ay	cl ean			
st ay				
str ay				
pr ay				

152	157	161	167	169
t oe	r oll	ouch	l ow	(cont.)
f oe	t oll	p ouch	fl ow	rocker
w oe	tr oll	c ouch	gl ow	painter
h oe	str oll	sl ouch	b ow	summer
	p ost		bl ow	
153	m ost	**162**	r ow	**170**
d ue	b olt	l oud	gr ow	s ing
c ue	j olt	pr oud	cr ow	k ing
h ue	c olt	cl oud	m ow	r ing
s ue	b oth		sn ow	str ing
	f orth	**163**	sh ow	sl ing
154	p ork	f ound	thr ow	w ing
w ild	p orch	p ound	b owl	sw ing
ch ild		r ound	own	th ing
b ind	**158**	gr ound	s own	br ing
bl ind	c ow	m ound	m own	
gr ind	n ow	b ound	bl own	**171**
m ind	b ow	s ound	fl own	jump ing
k ind	h ow	w ound	gr own	rest ing
f ind	r ow			runn ing
	pl ow	**164**	**168**	rubb ing
155	m ow	our	f our	help ing
s igh		s our	c our t	add ing
s igh t	**159**	fl our	c our se	wish ing
r igh t	owl		p our	swing ing
bright t	h owl	**165**		try ing
fl igh t	gr owl	m ouse	**169**	play ing
f igh t	f owl	h ouse	flower	read ing
m igh t		bl ouse	winter	
t igh t	**160**		sister	**Review**
n igh t	t own	**166**	rubber	yes
	d own	out	better	Henny
156	g own	p out	timber	cry
old	dr own	sp out	pitcher	aid
h old	br own	tr out	deeper	ail
g old	cr own	st out	hammer	aim
c old		sh out	older	rain
sc old		s outh	colder	hay
m old		m outh	dinner	each
s old				weak

183

Review (cont.)	173	178 (cont.)	Review	185 (cont.)
heal	kn it	th umb	gnat	packed
dream	kn ife	pl umb	knit	milked
bean	kn ight	l amb	wren	puffed
tear	kn ot		guide	
east	kn ob	**179**	buy	**186**
please	kn ee	holy	debt	v eil
freeze	kn eel	holly	limb	v ein
die	kn ow	later	holy	r ein
toad	kn ack	latter	silver	sk ein
oak	kn ock	filing	hero	
oat		filling		**187**
toast	**174**	pining	**182**	gr ief
oar	wr en	pinning	h ead	th ief
toe	wr ench	mating	r ead	ch ief
due	wr eck	matting	tr ead	br ief
wild	wr ap	summer	br ead	y ield
sigh	wr ite	carry	d eaf	sh ield
right	wr ing		m eant	
old	wr ist	**180**	sw eat	**188**
roll		sil ver	w ealth	eight
cow	**175**	vel vet		fr eight
owl	gu ide	win dow	**183**	w eight
town	gu est	sis ter	gr eat	w eigh
pouch	gu ess	pic nic	st eak	sl eigh
loud	ro gue		br eak	r eign
found	pla gue	**181**		
sour		he ro	**184**	**189**
mouse	**176**	sto ry	tint ed	th ey
pout	bu y	ba ker	jolt ed	pr ey
low	bu ild	mu sic	seat ed	wh ey
four		du ty	wick ed	
flower	**177**	ze ro	grad ed	**190**
jumping	de bt	pa per	coast ed	roared
	dou bt	gra vy	mend ed	prayed
172				snowed
gn at	**178**		**185**	cleaned
gn ash	li mb		baked	soured
si gn	co mb		ticked	crowed
	nu mb		choked	
			liked	

184

191	195	198	Review
t oo	oil	edge	head
t ool	b oil	hedge	great
r oof	s oil	pledge	tinted
pr oof	t oil	ridge	baked
st ool	c oin	bridge	veil
f ood	j oin	dodge	grief
l oose	n oise	lodge	eight
g oose		judge	they
sh oot	**196**		roared
ch oose	ice	**199**	too
	nice	ph onics	grew
192	price	or phan	good
gr ew	lace	sul phur	put
fl ew	face	ci pher	oil
thr ew	race	ele phant	ice
cr ew	fence	al phabet	age
dr ew	since		edge
	piece	**200**	phonics
193	niece	r ough	rough
g ood	voice	t ough	
h ood	city	l augh	
st ood	spicy	c ough	
h ook	juicy	tr ough	
w ool			
l ook	**197**		
	age		
194	rage		
p ut	sage		
p ull	page		
p uss	cage		
p ush	range		
f ull	danger		
b ush	manger		

CPSIA information can be obtained at www.ICGtesting.com
Printed in the USA
LVOW06s1716190514

386428LV00004B/1026/P